More Than Pleasure You

ALSO FROM SHAYLA BLACK

CONTEMPORARY ROMANCE

MORE THAN WORDS
More Than Want You
More Than Need You
More Than Love You
More Than Crave You
More Than Tempt You
More Than Pleasure You (novella)
Coming Soon:
More Than Dare You

THE WICKED LOVERS (Complete Series)

Wicked Ties
Decadent
Delicious
Surrender To Me
Belong To Me
"Wicked to Love" (novella)
Mine To Hold
"Wicked All The Way" (novella)
Ours To Love
Wicked All Night – Wicked and Dangerous Anthology
"Forever Wicked" (novella)
Theirs To Cherish
His to Take
Pure Wicked (novella)
Wicked for You
Falling in Deeper
"Dirty Wicked" (novella)
A Very Wicked Christmas (short story)
Holding on Tighter

Heavenly Rising Collection

The Choice
The Chase
Coming Soon:
The Commitment

THE HOPE SISTERS TRILOGY (Misadventures)
Misadventures of a Backup Bride
Misadventures with My Ex
Coming Soon:
My Best Friend's UnWedding

STANDALONE TITLES

Naughty Little Secret
Watch Me
Dangerous Boys And Their Toy
"Her Fantasy Men" – Four Play Anthology
A Perfect Match
Coming Soon:
Seduce the Bride (Sexy Short)

SEXY CAPERS

Bound And Determined
Strip Search
"Arresting Desire" – Hot In Handcuffs Anthology

HISTORICAL ROMANCE (as Shelley Bradley)

The Lady And The Dragon
One Wicked Night
Strictly Seduction
Strictly Forbidden

BROTHERS IN ARMS MEDIEVAL TRILOGY

His Lady Bride (Book 1)
His Stolen Bride (Book 2)
His Rebel Bride (Book 3)

**PARANORMAL ROMANCE
THE DOOMSDAY BRETHREN**

Tempt Me With Darkness
"Fated" (e-novella)
Seduce Me In Shadow
Possess Me At Midnight
"Mated" – Haunted By Your Touch Anthology
Entice Me At Twilight
Embrace Me At Dawn

More Than Pleasure You

A More Than Words Novella

By Shayla Black

1001 Dark Nights

EVIL EYE
CONCEPTS

More Than Pleasure You: A More Than Words Novella
Copyright 2019 Shelley Bradley LLC

ISBN: 978-1-970077-32-2

Foreword: Copyright 2014 M. J. Rose

Published by Evil Eye Concepts, Incorporated

ACKNOWLEDGMENTS FROM THE AUTHOR

Thanks so much to Liz Berry, MJ Rose, and Jillian Stein for welcoming me back into the 1,001 Dark Nights family after a few self-imposed years away. It means the world to me that you have such open arms and hearts, especially for this new series that means so much to me. You ladies are the best!

Sign up for the 1001 Dark Nights Newsletter
and be entered to win a Tiffany Key necklace.

There's a contest every month!

Go to www.1001DarkNights.com to subscribe.

**As a bonus, all subscribers can download
FIVE FREE exclusive books!**

ONE THOUSAND AND ONE DARK NIGHTS

Once upon a time, in the future…

*I was a student fascinated with stories and learning.
I studied philosophy, poetry, history, the occult, and
the art and science of love and magic. I had a vast
library at my father's home and collected thousands
of volumes of fantastic tales.*

*I learned all about ancient races and bygone
times. About myths and legends and dreams of all
people through the millennium. And the more I read
the stronger my imagination grew until I discovered
that I was able to travel into the stories... to actually
become part of them.*

*I wish I could say that I listened to my teacher
and respected my gift, as I ought to have. If I had, I
would not be telling you this tale now.
But I was foolhardy and confused, showing off
with bravery.*

*One afternoon, curious about the myth of the
Arabian Nights, I traveled back to ancient Persia to
see for myself if it was true that every day Shahryar
(Persian: شهریار, "king") married a new virgin, and then
sent yesterday's wife to be beheaded. It was written
and I had read, that by the time he met Scheherazade,
the vizier's daughter, he'd killed one thousand
women.*

*Something went wrong with my efforts. I arrived
in the midst of the story and somehow exchanged
places with Scheherazade – a phenomena that had
never occurred before and that still to this day, I
cannot explain.*

*Now I am trapped in that ancient past. I have
taken on Scheherazade's life and the only way I can
protect myself and stay alive is to do what she did to
protect herself and stay alive.*

*Every night the King calls for me and listens as I spin tales.
And when the evening ends and dawn breaks, I stop at a
point that leaves him breathless and yearning for more.
And so the King spares my life for one more day, so that
he might hear the rest of my dark tale.*

*As soon as I finish a story... I begin a new
one... like the one that you, dear reader, have before
you now.*

AUTHOR'S NOTE

There are infinite ways to tell someone you love them. Some of the most powerful don't require words at all. This was the truth rolling through my head when I first conceived of this series, writing about a love so complete that mere letters strung together to make sentences weren't an adequate communicator of those feelings. Music became my go-to choice.

I *love* music. I'm always immersed in it and spend hours a day with my earbuds plugged in. I write to music. I think to music. I even sleep to music. I was thrilled to incorporate songs into the story I felt were meaningful to the journey. I think of it this way: a movie has a soundtrack. Why shouldn't a book?

So I created one.

Some of the songs I've selected will be familiar. Some are old. Some are newer. Some popular. Some even obscure. They all just fit (in my opinion) and came straight from the heart. I listened to many of these songs as I wrote the book.

For maximum understanding (and feels), I seriously recommend becoming familiar with these songs and either playing them or rolling them around in your head as you read. Due to copyright laws, I can't use exact lyrics, but where needed I tried to give you the gist of those most meaningful to this story. I've even made it simple for you to give these songs a listen by creating a Spotify playlist.

Hugs and happy reading!

The Approaching Night - Philip Wesley
Embraced - Paul Cardall
My Immortal - Evanescence
Shut Up and Dance - Walk The Moon
Isn't She Lovely - Stevie Wonder
Marry You - Bruno Mars

Additionally, the events of *More Than Pleasure* you coincide with the gap in time toward the end of *More Than Tempt You*. If you've read that book, you may recognize those references. If you haven't read *More Than Tempt You*, don't worry. You don't need to read that story to understand this one. Hope you enjoy!

CHAPTER ONE

Tuesday, January 9
Maui

Stephen

"What were you thinking? I can't conjure up a hot fiancé out of thin air."

Who the hell is that?

Despite the fact my head hurts like a bitch, I look away from the calm blue ocean, glancing over my shoulder and above the rim of my sunglasses at whoever invaded my rented vacation house uninvited. The source of the unfamiliar female voice isn't hard to find. The blonde bustling around the living room fluffing pillows on the sofa has a cell phone pressed to her ear—and a really nice ass.

"You're not supposed to ask who I'm dating now," she insists. "We broke up."

Is her ex sniffing around? I can't see the blonde's face, but the language of her very fine body tells me she's annoyed.

"I know you're in a rough spot, Finn. And I know your wedding is this weekend. But you can't ask me to fake-date any of your friends, even for a night. I know them all way too well. More importantly, so do your parents."

The douchecanoe really just asked her to lie to everyone at his wedding by faking an engagement with some guy she doesn't like? I haven't caught a glimpse of the blonde's face, but nothing I've seen leads me to believe she needs help finding someone new.

Yeah, I shouldn't eavesdrop, and she clearly has no idea I'm sitting on the lanai, but even if I had the energy to get up, I couldn't manage it clandestinely now.

She tosses her hand in the air. "It's not like I hang out in a singles mecca where I can pick up someone for the hell of it and decide to get married three weeks later."

"Sorry." She pauses, then sighs. "No. I really don't care how you met Dana. You and I were never going to last, so I'm happy you found someone to spend your life with. I just wish you hadn't told your parents I'd be bringing my nonexistent new fiancé."

He did *what?*

As she paces the room, she listens, shaking her head. "I get that, but it's not my fault they like me better than Dana."

Suddenly, she holds the phone away from her ear. "Don't yell. I know. Apology accepted, but I'm working today. We have a guest arriving tomorrow. I'll see what I can do once I'm off tonight, all right? In the meantime, if my Prince Charming just happens to appear, I'll let you know. Bye."

With a sigh, she ends the call, pockets the phone, then pivots for the kitchen.

Halfway through her turn, she spots me on the lounger through the open door and gasps. "Oh, my god. I didn't expect anyone here. You overheard my conversation, didn't you?"

My first full glimpse of her is a TKO to my solar plexus. Her big brown eyes and her kissable pink mouth compete for the most mesmerizing feature on her stunning, makeup-free face. Disheveled golden hair spills around her slender shoulders, one slim section swaying in a bohemian braid with the breeze, brushing her mouthwatering breasts, which are hugged by a form-fitting white T-shirt. Shapely tanned thighs extend from brief denim cutoffs and end in bare feet decorated with cheery aqua polish and a toe ring.

She's not my usual kind of woman, but she's fucking gorgeous.

Why would anyone ever think she needs help finding a date?

"Hard not to," I admit.

She closes her eyes. "Are you our next guest, Mr. Lund?"

I nod, then regret it instantly, holding a hand to my aching head. "Just Stephen."

"I'm both very sorry and incredibly embarrassed." She heads outside, hand outstretched. "I'm Skye."

The name fits her—earthy, natural, sun-kissed.

I slide my palm against hers, loving her so-soft skin. At her touch, something new hits me. I can't define it. It's more than a vibe, more than mere interest. Even more than simple lust, though I feel that, too. "Nice to meet you."

She ends our handshake and slips into professional mode. "Welcome to the Aloha Rainbow house. I'll be the property caretaker and your chef during your stay. I'm sorry the place wasn't ready. I was told you wouldn't be arriving until tomorrow."

"That was the plan…until I got a concussion. A friend of mine called the owners and arranged for me to check in a day early so I could recover in peace." Bless Bethany for realizing I need some quiet and solitude— and not just to recover from my injury. Plus, my whack on the head buys me an extra day to evaluate whether this property is right for commercial development.

"Oh, my gosh. I'm so sorry to hear that. Can I get you something? Assist you in any way?" Then she winces as if she worries her voice might be too loud and drops to a whisper. "Do you want me to stop talking?"

I manage a smile. "You're fine, but I spent last night in the hospital. The mattress was uncomfortable and the food was lousy."

"That sounds horrible." She rushes forward to take my suitcase. "Would you like to go to bed?"

"Wow, you move fast. I mean, we *just* met. Normally, I'd at least buy you dinner first, but…" I wink her way.

Her big eyes slide shut again. "Every time I open my mouth today, I seem to insert my foot."

I laugh because she's fun to tease. "I knew you weren't hitting me up for sex. Clearly, you've already got problems."

"Those aren't important. Let's get you settled. Should I ready the house for someone else to join you?"

"Nope. It's just me. I thought my friend might come." I tried to persuade Bethany to stay since she and Clint are breaking up…maybe. In truth, she loves him, and I'm beginning to suspect I misjudged the guy and that he genuinely loves her, too. "But no, so I've got the place all to myself."

"We've got thirty-six hundred square feet of interior space and twenty-four hundred dedicated to our waterfront lanais, so it's a lot of house for one person, but you'll find it incredibly relaxing. The beach is very private. Besides the property owners and me, no one will have access during your stay. Have you taken a tour of the house and grounds yet?"

"Just online."

"Would you like one now or would you rather I show you upstairs and give you some privacy?"

I left everything and everyone behind in Manhattan to find some much-needed perspective. Besides the fact this place has amazing oceanfront views, I chose it because I got a phone call from David Chang, an important, long-time client, two days ago. He's looking for the perfect property on Maui to build skyscraping hotels. This parcel of private land seems to have great potential. I told him I'd check it out and report back. I haven't clued my dad in about this potential opportunity. I need to decide how to handle that—and everything else—going forward. That's part of why I'm here. It's an added bonus that this luxury rental is only ten minutes from my half-sister, whom I'm still getting to know.

But now that I've met Skye, I'm not as eager for alone-time to ruminate. She's hot and her problems are interesting.

Maybe they only seem that way because you're avoiding your own?

"No, thanks." A tour is irrelevant since none of what's here will be left if this deal goes through. It's kind of a shame since this place is amazing, at least what I've seen. "But you said something about food?"

"I cook breakfast, hors d'oeuvres, and dinner every day except Monday. Just name your preferred times. Also let me know if you have any food sensitivities. Are you vegan, gluten-free, lactose-intol—"

"I'm not picky, just hungry."

"All right." She glances at her phone. "It's a little after three. How about I make you a snack to tide you over until dinner?"

"Thank you."

She nods, then lifts my bag. "I'll take this upstairs to the master bedroom."

"I got it." The gentleman in me prods me to my feet to take my suitcase from her.

A wave of dizziness flattens me, and I stumble back on my ass.

The unexpected weakness rankles my male pride, but the sympathy that crosses her face does other things to me. I've never been fascinated by the sheer expressiveness of a woman's eyes, but hers give me an interesting glimpse into her soul—goodness, intelligence, and a streak of something wild.

Against my better judgment, I want to explore that.

"How bad does your head hurt?" she asks.

"Like someone gave a metal-thrash drummer a double dose of speed, a sturdy hammer, and a steel trash can lid."

She winces. "Sounds terrible. Do you have any medications I should give you?"

"The hospital dosed me with acetaminophen before discharging me. I also have some painkillers I can take with food if my head hurts too much."

"Then let's put something in your stomach." She sets my suitcase aside and helps me to my feet.

I feel ridiculous for needing to lean on Skye, but the dizziness is no joke. Besides, I like her petite curves pressed against me. My head might be protesting, but the rest of me is perking up with interest.

After all, I'm injured, not dead.

"Do you want me to close the blinds?" she asks as she guides me inside, across the living room. "Make it darker?"

It would probably be better for me but… "I'd rather not give up this view."

She smiles in understanding as she settles me on a barstool at the kitchen peninsula, then rushes to pull out arugula, an herbed cheese, thinly sliced steak, balsamic, and a baguette. "Did you have a car accident?"

"No. A guy tried to bash in my head with a baseball bat."

Her eyes widen as she starts chopping. "Someone attacked you?"

"I was defending a friend. It didn't end as well as I'd hoped." For anyone. But Bethany is all right. That's what's important. "Don't worry. I'll be fine."

"I'm also a licensed massage therapist. If you'd like an hour of my time…"

The lure of relief—and yeah, her touch—is too much to resist. "How about after whatever you're making?"

"Crostini. Sure. I have a table I can set up on the lanai." She grins as she assembles the food on a baking sheet. "You can have a romantic sunset massage for one."

While I'd love to get her naked, too, I'm in no shape to do anything but smile back. "I'll take it."

I watch Skye toss together the small meat-covered slices of bread, then she shoves them under the broiler. "Is your friend okay?"

"She's fine." Or she will be once she realizes that everything that happened last night was for the best. "I'll call her tomorrow to check in. She's going through a lot right now."

"Are you close?"

"We've known each other since we were kids. Bethany is a good person who's been dealt a rotten hand." I hate that she's leaving the island, but I get why. In her shoes, I'd probably do the same.

"I'm sure she appreciates you."

Bethany isn't in a place to appreciate anything right now, so I just shrug. "What can I say? I'm an overall good guy. I care about the people around me. So why don't we talk about your problem?"

Skye stiffens as she removes the crostini from the broiler. "That's not necessary."

"So you've already got a solution?" I challenge, knowing full well she doesn't.

She grabs a spatula from a nearby drawer, then plates the crostini, spreading fresh arugula on top and drizzling everything with balsamic while ignoring my question.

"Finn is your ex, right? His parents don't like his bride-to-be, Dana." I frown. "Why would he invite you to his wedding?"

"He didn't; his parents did. They've been good friends with my mom and dad for years. But since they retired and moved to Florida, I have to go and represent our family."

"Ah. So Finn's folks invited you to the wedding, hoping...what? That he'll see you and change his mind about marrying the 'wrong girl.' But since you're over each other, he told them you found someone new. And now they're expecting you to bring your new fiancé. Only you don't have one. Does that sum up the situation?"

She pushes the plate toward me. "Eat."

I dive in with gusto. Pleasure melts my taste buds. Yes, I'm hungry, but I've also dined at my fair share of swanky five-star restaurants, so I know good food when I taste it. "This is amazing."

"I'm glad you like it. I'd offer you wine, but in your condition that's not a good idea. Water?"

"Please. Why don't you drink the wine for me?"

Skye hesitates. "I'm on the job."

"I won't tell." When she still looks reluctant, I press on. "Look, I'm not trying to get you tipsy. As you pointed out, I can't drink tonight, so I'd like to enjoy you enjoying the wine."

She cocks her head and studies me. "You're serious."

"I never say things I don't mean."

As I take another hearty bite, she fixes me a glass of water with a lemon wedge. "One glass. What the heck?"

While I hoover another slab of the savory toasted bread into my mouth, she uncorks the bottle of red, pours some into a stem, and sips with a sigh of satisfaction. "That's really good."

She sounds surprised.

"You've never tasted it?"

"No. I buy it on Dean and Erma's behalf for the guests. They're the owners. But you probably knew that. They must have checked you in."

"About ten this morning, yes. And I really hadn't much moved from that chaise since."

"No wonder you were hungry. Can I make you something else before dinner?"

"This is great for now."

I watch her sip more vino. When she moans—unconsciously?—then licks the wine from her lips, I wish like hell my head didn't feel so close to exploding so I could turn on the charm and see what the night might bring.

"I'll go get the massage table." She disappears, then returns a moment later with a fluffy white robe and helps me to my feet, guiding me to a half bath off the living room. "Change here. I'll set everything up and come back for you."

When Skye shuts the door behind me, I shimmy out of my clothes, holding on to the basin for balance. I'm not used to being physically unable to do anything. I have a voracious gym habit. I play racquetball, run half-marathons, and dabble in triathlons for fun. Not being able to take off my own pants without wobbling is fucking frustrating.

Finally, I manage to get naked and wrap the robe around me, then open the door. Skye is tucking the last of the soft white sheets around the massage table.

It takes some doing, but I make my way to her. "That looks like heaven."

"I would have helped you." She tsks at me before taking another sip of wine, then hitting the button on a nearby speaker to start the spa music.

"I'm good." In truth, I'm feeling a little better after food.

"Go ahead and get on the table, face down. Take your time. I'll be back in a few."

Skye bustles away. My stare glues itself to the golden waves of her hair brushing her back, above the sensual sway of her ass. I didn't expect to be so intrigued by anyone at this secluded slice of paradise. I especially didn't expect to meet someone like her. My usual hookups are ballbusters in pencil skirts and stilettos. I enjoy melting women with strong wills into tiny, moaning puddles. But I'm not looking for a fling now. And forget relationships. I've got too much going on. Yet...when I lay eyes on this woman, I'm tempted to make an exception.

Without my sunglasses, I squint against the afternoon sun as I peel off my robe and get supine on the massage table, thankfully managing not to fall and embarrass myself. Finally, I get comfortable face down, under the covers, forehead in the cradle. Ocean waves crash, lulling me to a more relaxed state. A warm breeze skates over me.

This is another reason I came to Hawaii. In New York, I'd be freezing my balls off in January, cursing the arctic wind coming off the Hudson and counting the days until threats of snow no longer dog the weather forecast. Right now, I'm perfectly comfortable in my birthday suit, shielded only by a sheet and light blanket. It really is paradise.

"Ready?" Skye asks from a few feet away.

"Beyond."

"Excellent."

I don't know this woman, and yet I hear an audible smile in her voice. It's a genuine desire to help me. In my cutthroat line of work, assistance always comes with a price.

"So, Skye, what are you charging me for this?"

She pauses for the briefest of moments. "Nothing."

"I read the materials Erma emailed me. It mentioned that massage was by appointment only and that there was an associated fee."

"Normally, but this one is on me since you stepped up to defend a friend. That's amazing."

Skye is *giving* me this massage when she isn't even the person I helped? "I just did what any friend would."

"That's not true, but the fact you think so says a lot."

She makes me sound like some sort of saint. Nothing could be further from the truth.

"Is the music too loud?" she asks as she folds the covers down to my hips.

"Actually, it's nice." I'm usually a hip-hop and R&B guy, so not hating the instrumentals is a surprise. As one song flows into the next, I ask, "What is it?"

"The song that just ended is 'The Approaching Night' by Philip Wesley. The next is 'Embraced' by Paul Cardall." Then she laughs. "You've never heard of either, I'm sure."

"No."

"I work for two octogenarians. If you want to know anything about Big Bands or easy listening, just ask me."

"I don't know whether to give you my sympathy or congratulations."

She laughs. "Maybe both. Do you want your pain meds before we start?"

Right now, I don't want anything that will make me loopy. I'd rather talk to Skye. "No thanks. Maybe before bed."

"Sure. Do you have any problem areas you'd like me to focus on? What kind of pressure do you prefer?"

We talk back and forth, and she agrees to give me a deep-tissue massage, focused on my neck, shoulders, and lower back. Since I visit one of Manhattan's most exclusive spas every two weeks for ninety minutes of expert stress relief under some of the deftest hands in the city, I'm not expecting Skye to do me much good. To my surprise, she's firm without being harsh. She seems to intuitively know where my knots are and how to alleviate them without causing discomfort.

When her palm covers my nape and her fingers massage my seemingly concrete neck, I melt onto the table with a groan. "You're fabulous at this."

"Thank you."

"You sure I can't pay you?"

"Positive."

This argument isn't worth having, so I'm going to move on to something more important—or that's my plan until her nimble thumbs manipulate under my shoulder blades, relieving a shitload of tension.

As she slides her digits down the line of my aching spine, I groan. "Yes, right there. Oh…"

Dutifully, she digs in and wrests another moan from me. If I'm honest, it's not the reason I'd like to be groaning with her, but hopefully I'll be capable of more than flirtation tomorrow.

"You carry a lot of tension in your neck and mid-back."

"High-stress job."

"What do you do, Mr. Lund?"

"Just Stephen."

Skye fans her knuckles under my shoulder blades, eliciting another raw sound of pleasure. "Okay, what do you do, just Stephen?"

Isn't that a good question? I don't know the answer anymore.

"Do you want the short or long version?"

"Whatever you want to share. But we've got an hour...and I'm curious."

"I work with my dad. We have a global acquisitions and investments business. Any chance you've heard of Colossus Investment Corporation?"

"No. Sorry."

It's a venerable Wall Street institution, but it's been very private and reserved for the uber wealthy—until now. "Don't be. Not everyone has. We're set to launch our IPO this summer and we need all hands on deck, but I recently met my dad's illegitimate daughter, whom he refuses to recognize. I have my suspicions about his reasons for that and I hope I'm wrong, but he's being a raging asshole, so I'm deciding now whether I want to continue growing the business with him or branch out on my own. On the one hand, this has been my livelihood for years. I've helped expand this operation and planned a lot of this initial stock offering. Helming Colossus has been my dream. On the other, I've lost a lot of respect for my father. So I'm here, trying to decide where my future lies. Aren't you sorry you asked?"

"No, but I'm sorry to hear all that."

"It is what it is. But I figure that, since I know some of your business, I'd level the playing field by telling you some of mine." And maybe I'm a little subversive in hoping that if we hit it off now, she'll be open to things happening between us once my head doesn't feel as if it might split open.

"Thanks. Weirdly, knowing your life isn't perfect either makes me feel less self-conscious."

"Oh, my life is an utter shit show. One-hundred-percent. So..." I glance at her over my shoulder as she digs her dainty elbow into the small of my back, wrenching another throaty groan from me. "God, if you keep that up the neighbors are going to think we're back here getting freaky."

Her melodic laugh buoys me. "You're in luck. Our long-term renters are away for the holidays." Then she drops her voice to a whisper. "But between you and me, they're not quiet about the fact they're pretty freaky themselves."

"Good to know. But you're so amazing at this, I'm going to need you to massage me again. A whole lot. I'm happy to pay you outright, but if you're helping me with my problem, I feel like I should help you with yours. Why don't you let me take you to Finn's wedding?"

She freezes. "You can't be serious."

"Why not? You need a date, and I can make that happen. C'mon… I'll be the best fake fiancé you've ever had, baby. What do you say?"

* * * *

"I must be crazy," Skye murmurs as we sit facing each other on the stools at the breakfast bar the following morning.

Since she agreed to let me be her fake fiancé for the weekend and my head no longer throbs, we're going to spend the next two days getting to know each other. Score for me.

I probably shouldn't pursue her…but I'm not inclined to stop myself, especially when she looks totally edible. Today, she's wearing another pair of sexy cutoffs and a crop top that clings low on her breasts, hugs her ribs, and flashes me her flat belly.

I try not to stare…but I fail miserably. "Not crazy, crafty. We'll convince Finn's parents that you're off the market, and hopefully they'll start accepting Dana. Then you and your ex can both move on. Everyone is happy."

"I sure hope so. Finn and I have always been friends, but we broke up months ago, and his mother especially won't give up on the notion that if she gives us the right nudge we'll get back together. It's never going to happen."

"Why don't Finn's parents like Dana?"

"Wait until you meet her."

So she either doesn't want to color my opinion or talk bad about her ex's new squeeze. I respect that.

"We have roughly seventy-two hours between now and the wedding to give each other a crash course about our lives." It's the only way we'll convince people we're engaged.

"I'm nervous."

I take her hand. To reassure her, yes. But it's also hard to resist touching her. "We've got this. I searched the Internet for things prospective spouses should know about each other, so we'll cover those. I emailed you the names and bios of my family members, as well as some bits about my childhood, schooling, and background."

"I got it, Stephen Montgomery Lund. How cool that you were born in Paris and have visited six of the seven continents. I've only been off Hawaii twice." She sighs wistfully as she leans in to prop her chin on her fist.

Holy cleavage.

I struggle to keep my tongue in my mouth and my thoughts on track. "You're actually from here?"

She nods. "My dad was stationed on Oahu when I was born. I was a later-in-life baby, but when I was four the military made noise about relocating us to El Paso. He got out for my mom because staying in Hawaii meant the world to her."

Wow. The man switched careers to make his wife happy. While it sounds impractical, the wistful expression on Skye's face tells me she respects the hell out of her dad for his decision.

"And also because that place is nicknamed Hell Paso for a reason."

That makes me laugh. "So what brought you all to Maui?"

"It was quieter here. And Dad could make a good living giving tourists helicopter tours."

"Too bad he moved. I would have liked seeing the island from the air."

"I miss my parents, but my grandmother isn't well and couldn't leave her home, so they went to take care of her."

Family looking out for family. That's something else I've never experienced. As far as I know, my dad stuck his own mother in a home and never visited. That seems cold since the woman gave birth to him.

"I'm curious… Since you've lived here your whole life, can you hula?"

She scoffs. "Any self-respecting girl from the islands can."

Oh, I'd love to see that. "Show me?"

She rolls her eyes. "Maybe later."

I'm going to turn that maybe into a yes. "All right. Since you've only been off Hawaii twice, tell me one place you're dying to go."

"Vegas." Her eyes light up. "It looks so cool on the internet. I want to take a gondola ride at the Venetian, watch the water fountain show at the Bellagio, walk the Strip, catch some shows, and…oh, eat at one of those celebrity chef restaurants."

I've done all those things, but I'd do them again to see that wide-eyed look of wonder on her face. "Don't blame you."

She gives me a self-deprecating grimace. "I probably sound ridiculous. And touristy. Sorry. I'm focusing now. I'll put together my background information and send it to you as soon as we're done here."

"Perfect." I'm not worried about the simple facts. It's the other things that can trip us up that concern me. "Do we have a song? Something we can ask the deejay at the wedding to play for us?"

"No." She shakes her head with a hint of contempt. "I'm not that kind of girl."

I raise a brow. "What kind is that?"

"Sentimental. I live in the moment. I can't fix yesterday and I can't control tomorrow." She shrugs.

"You don't plan?"

"Not a lot. It's as exciting as a dental appointment and as pointless as a concrete parachute." She shrugs. "It almost never works."

Her attitude blows my mind since I've made a very good living in helping people plan for the future. "Interesting perspective."

"You think I'm wrong."

"Yep." I'm not going to argue…but I'm also not going to lie.

"You wouldn't be the first person. How did we meet?"

"At a bar?"

Skye wrinkles her nose. "I don't do bars—or random hookups."

"Fair enough." I respect her for that. "Where could I have met you?"

"Most likely? At Honolua Bay, surfing."

"I don't know how to surf." It's one of the few sports I haven't tried, but I wouldn't mind. "At least not yet."

"I can teach you."

"I'd love that." It sounds interesting, sure. I'd also kill to see her in a bikini.

"Maybe tomorrow. If that's our cover story, you should know a little bit about it before the wedding."

"You're on."

"Since you're a novice, we'll have to tell everyone we met at Kihei

Cove. I don't go there often, but enough that no one will question the story."

"All right. When did we meet? How long have we been dating? Have we intentionally been keeping it a secret?"

She looks a tad worried, as if she's realizing that creating a convincing narrative is going to be harder than she first thought. "It has to be fast. I dropped into a birthday bash Finn's parents threw for him back in September. They asked me then if I was dating anyone. I wasn't, so I said no."

"Maybe you didn't want to tell them your personal business."

She shakes her head. "They've known me since I was five. And they'd know I was lying. Apparently, I'm terrible at it. I can't keep a straight face."

And we have to fool almost everyone she knows?

"Good thing we're going to a wedding. People are typically happy, so smiling won't seem weird. But maybe you should let me talk."

"Are you a good liar?" She grins as if the notion of getting some dirt on me is appealing.

"I was one hell of a teenage rebel. It's a miracle I never got caught or arrested...and we'll leave it there."

She laughs, the sound so light and melodious it makes me weirdly happy, too. In fact, I love knowing I put that grin on her face.

"Then you should definitely talk. I'll smile and nod."

"Perfect. How about we say we met in October while I was here for a client meeting and that we've continued dating whenever I visited the island?"

"That works. I started seeing less of Finn's parents around that time since they got tied up with the wedding after he suddenly proposed to Dana."

I nod. "So where was our first date?"

"You seem like an upscale sort of guy. You probably would have taken me to someplace like Merriman's, not knowing it's not my thing."

I shake my head. "I would have made it a point to learn something about you before I asked you out. Besides, I don't live here, so I would have asked for your recommendation. What would you have said?"

"There's this hole-in-the-wall barbecue place in Kihei that's to die for. It's my favorite."

"Okay, so I took you there after you tried to teach me to surf."

"That's plausible, but how did we get serious enough to get engaged if you don't actually live here?"

Good point. "Let's say I've been here off and on for business most of the fall, but stayed over the holidays to be with family who lives nearby. And with you, of course." It's not a perfect story. If anyone looks too deep, they'll be able to punch holes in it. But if this only has to float for a couple of hours, it will hold.

"You said your half-sister lives around here?"

"Yeah, Nia. Until recently, I tried to get a deal done with her boss— now husband—Evan Cook. The brilliant bastard decided not to sell at the last minute."

Skye nibbles her lip. "When I'm nervous, I won't remember all this."

"Another reason for you to let me talk. I'm good on my feet. Years of making boring business presentations and having to answer questions on the fly."

"That works for me. Um…what's our engagement story? How did you propose?"

"Are you saying you're not the liberated sort of woman who would pop the question to her man?" When she cocks her head as if she's actually considering it, I step in. "Please don't say yes."

"You're old fashioned?"

"When it comes to who should do the proposing, totally."

That makes her laugh again. "All right. So you proposed. I obviously said yes."

"Obviously," I drawl. "Speaking of which…"

When I pull out a ring from my pocket, she gasps. "Where did you get that?"

"Don't worry. I didn't actually go ring shopping," I assure her. "Last night, I called a friend of a friend who deals in high-quality simulations. He overnighted this loaner to me. It's two carats of cushion-cut moissanite, a diamond alternative."

"It looks so real," she breathes.

"That's the point. I didn't think you'd want anything too big or elaborate…"

She shakes her head. "Anything more would seem gaudy to me. This is perfect."

It shouldn't matter what Skye thinks since she's only going to wear this for the weekend, but I'm ridiculously relieved that I guessed her style right.

"Glad you like it." When she reaches for the ring, I curl it into my fist. "Hang on. We have to do this properly."

She raises a brow. "What do you mean?"

I hop off my barstool, turn her to face me, drop down to one knee—and get a great glimpse up her sleek, sun-kissed thighs. "Skye…what the hell is your last name?"

"Ingram."

"Middle name?"

"Nicole." She giggles. "Your mockposal is off to a great start."

"Shh," I admonish with a grin. "Skye Nicole Ingram, we've known each other for a whole twenty-four hours. In that time, you've made me smile, made me think, and—I admit—made me want to kiss you breathless. You've amused, befuddled, and intrigued me. Most of all, you've made me glad we've chosen this weekend together. If you say yes, I'll be the best fake fiancé ever—listening, laughing, and loving you—from now until Sunday morning. Will you do me the honor of fake marrying me?"

Her giggles dissolve into outright laughter. "Yes."

"Excellent." I stand and wrap my fingers around her wrist, carefully guiding the simulated diamond onto her ring finger, where it winks and sparkles, looking as if it was made just for her.

"You've got a goofy side."

"Me?" I act shocked…but she's right. I kind of do. Not that I'd ever show my father. Bethany and a few others know, but it feels nice to be myself around Skye. Despite how hot I am to touch her, I'm surprisingly comfortable around her, too. "Maybe a little."

She rolls her eyes. "Now that the corny proposal is over, when should we say our engagement actually happened? Where? And why?"

"December? We would have been dating for two months by then."

She pauses, thinks. "That's fast, but… We have to say it was late in the month. I ran into Finn's parents on Christmas Eve while I was out shopping. They would have noticed an engagement ring."

"How about we say I proposed on New Year's Eve?"

"That works. I was at home alone, but no one knows that except my parents. The good news is, Finn's folks haven't talked to mine since before the holidays. I'll call Mom and Dad and tell them to play along with our engagement. They'll back me up."

"Good. The where we got engaged... Why not here?"

"Sure. The people who had rented this place for the week had to cancel at the last minute, due to a family emergency. So you could have swooped in and come to ring in the New Year. The view is great, as you know. And it's totally romantic..."

Her wistful sigh gets me thinking. "Is romance important to you?"

"It might be nice someday. No one has ever truly been romantic with me."

"Not even Finn?"

"Especially not Finn. One of the reasons we didn't work out was because we'd been friends for too long. It just felt...weird."

"I get that. I've been there, too," I admit. "So why did we get engaged?"

"Don't most people get engaged because they're in love?"

"Probably." But I've seen tons of business and old-money marriages. "But maybe you're saying 'I do' for the cash flow. I'm not a poor man."

She recoils. "I don't know how many zeros are in your bank account and I don't care. If I only wanted money, I would have married Finn. In college, he and one of his buddies developed a dating app, then sold it three years later for a ridiculous amount of money. He'll never have to work again. But I've always sworn that *if* I ever get married, it will be for love."

"So we have to behave like we're head over heels and be totally convincing."

"Pretty much."

"We'll manage," I promise. "You know, you're an adorable contradiction. You claim you're not sentimental, but you're a romantic?"

"Not the same thing. I don't cling to what was, especially if it's not working. But I'm all about the things in your life having meaning, and marriage should be one of the deepest connections of all." She pauses to gather her words. "I don't expect it to make anything easier. But I would rather go through the hard times with someone I love than have a perfectly carefree life alone."

Her words hit me like a two-ton weight. Isn't that the life I've had? Effortless, silver-spoon, and utterly meaningless?

I sit back, stare, and turn that over mentally.

"What?" Skye blinks up at me.

It sounds both ridiculous and hokey to say that, with one sentence, she's made me examine my life. But she kind of did.

"Nothing. We should get through some of these questions I Googled." I grab my phone, momentarily glad I have something to get lost in besides her. "What do you like to do in your free time, besides surf?"

"Meditation and yoga, volunteer at the animal shelter, hang out with friends. You?"

"I don't really have free time." I've devoted my life to making money, and I'm fucking good at it. Not spending every day hustling is foreign to me. Even now, I'm supposed to be vacationing, but I feel restless and agitated. Off balance.

"Tell me about your friends."

Besides Bethany, I have a lot of business acquaintances…and almost as many hookups. But people I actually care about. The ones I'd go out on a limb for? My ride-or-dies? Not really. Funny, I never realized that. Or did I, at least subconsciously? Maybe that's why I've been trying to establish a relationship with Nia, despite our father's threats and protests.

"I've been pretty focused on my career."

She frowns at me. "You should work to live, not live to work."

Not in the Lund household. "I didn't get that memo."

"Well, admitting the problem is the first step. And if you need a friend, I'm here."

Would Skye really open her life and let me in, just like that? Sure, I'm helping her, but I had to convince her to let me. I'm pretty good at reading people, and she isn't merely telling me what I want to hear. She won't conveniently forget this conversation once Finn's parents are off her back. She genuinely means it.

If we were in a bar and I was looking for an opening to proposition her, I'd use this moment as an opportunity. I'd take her hand, draw her closer, whisper things I knew she wanted to hear. She's given me plenty of clues about how to win her over. But I don't. Instead, I swallow against my suddenly tight throat and nod. "Thank you."

"Of course."

I glance at the list on my phone again. "Introvert or extrovert?"

"Introvert. I'm not super shy, but I don't like big crowds. And I definitely like alone time."

"I relate. I'm an extroverted introvert. I can turn on in crowds. Public speaking is a breeze to me since I've learned to smile and be gregarious, but I'm always itching to get home and decompress. The whole thing exhausts me."

She nods as if she totally understands. "What else?"

"Morning person or night owl?"

"Neither. I flow with the natural rhythm of my body." She hesitates, eyes narrowed. "You're a morning person, aren't you?"

"I'm usually in the gym by five a.m., out by six-thirty, and at my first meeting before eight. Most often I get to bed around midnight."

"That's not enough sleep. Do you catch up on weekends?"

"No. My schedule is the same seven days a week. I don't have an eight-to-five job."

Her frown becomes a scowl. "So those continents you've visited...all for business?"

"Yes. This is the first vacation I've taken since I went to work for my dad."

Skye looks stunned—and not in a good way. "We're definitely going to make sure you enjoy it."

For as long as I'm here scouting the property? Until I figure out what to do about the craptastic problems in my life? "Great. Do you have any odd talents?"

"Not really. I haven't met a craft I didn't like. I can quilt, stitch, make pottery, create stained glass, garden..."

Nice. If my mom wanted anything like that done, she hired it out. She was way too busy climbing the social ladder to bother getting her hands dirty. "Now I feel really untalented. Unless you call smooth-talking corporate executives and third-world leaders a special ability, I've got nothing."

"Seriously? You must have played sports in high school."

"I swam and ran track, played a little baseball. Mostly, I whizzed through schoolwork so I could spend my evenings learning my dad's business from the ground up."

She hesitates. "Would leaving it behind be like walking away from everything you've ever known?"

More like losing an arm or a leg. "Yeah."

"So...it's not an easy decision."

"No." I've also avoided thinking about it because I can't picture a life outside of New York. I've traveled the world, but I've always considered the city home.

"Are you really sure you want to mess with my ridiculous problem?"

"If I don't, will Finn's mom keep hounding you?"

She sighs. "Probably. He and I both thought she would let it go after his engagement. Instead she's gotten more insistent. I worry that even after he and Dana have said their I-do's, if I don't look attached she'll try to convince me to wait for his marriage to fail. I feel bad for Finn. He just wants to be happy."

"So you think having a fiancé will finally convince her to back off?"

"I hope. In her head, I'm all alone, and Finn is only marrying Dana because he's a stubborn dumb ass. But if she sees I've moved on, too, I have to think she'll give up."

"Tell me one thing that will *really* convince her you're no longer interested in Finn."

Skye pauses. "I haven't thought about it like that... Probably behaving unlike the way I did with Finn."

"What do you mean?"

"She was always encouraging us to kiss and hold hands. She would give us romantic weekends away. Once, when I made an offhanded mention that my period was late, she asked me—gleefully—if there was any chance I was pregnant. I didn't have the heart to tell her no."

No chance at all? "Not to be too personal, but did you ever have sex with Finn?"

"No. Maybe he might have tried harder if I had been more receptive. But mostly I think we both felt pushed into the relationship."

"So you and I have to act like we can't keep our hands off each other?"

"Probably." She winces. "Yeah. Sorry."

"It's not a problem." At all. I reach for her hand—and frown when Skye jolts. "But if we're going to convince anyone, especially people who have known you for years, that we're getting married because we're desperately in love, you can't jump when I touch you. We have to leave them thinking that we barely managed to roll out of bed for the wedding and that we'll probably roll right back in as soon as we're alone."

"You're right. It's just, um...been a while since anyone kissed me. I don't count Finn."

"How long?"

She pauses. "Two years and some change."

Whoa. Skye deserves to be kissed well and often by someone

desperate to make love to that pillowy pink mouth with abandon. Hell, yeah, I'll volunteer. And if it's been that long since anyone has kissed her, how long since someone has taken her to bed and pleasured her? I don't ask—but I'm really fucking curious. "I did not see that coming."

"Embarrassing, right?"

I shake my head. "No."

"You're being nice." She slides off the stool and onto her feet, shaking slightly. "So you think we should wing the whole PDA thing...or maybe practice a little?"

"Definitely practice." I can't help but grin. "A lot."

Skye bites her soft lip. "You're probably right."

I am. And that makes her very nervous.

"No maybe about it." I flash what I hope is a reassuring smile, not one that divulges the fact that I woke up with an aching cock and her on my mind.

"Okay, how should we—"

I stop her awkward, breathless question by kicking away from my stool. The legs drag across the tile as I stand. That's the only sound in the room besides the distant crash of surf and her suddenly rapid breathing.

"Come here." I crook my finger.

She blinks, then slowly shuffles toward me. The moment she's close enough, I circle an arm around her waist, wrap my hand around her nape, and pull her flush against me.

Her shocked little gasp sends a thrill zipping through me. We're nearly nose to nose. My mouth hovers a breath above hers. And I don't give her time to get nervous or second-guess herself. Nope. I dip my head and seize her lips.

The moment our mouths meet, an electric sizzle jolts through my veins—hot, pervasive, shocking. Sure, I usually enjoy kissing, but this... It's more. It's beyond. I don't bother letting her get used to me or learning her slowly. I can't seem to downshift or back off. I want this too much.

Between one heartbeat and the next, the desire I've restrained since she walked in the door with a cup of coffee and a nervous smile comes off its leash. I barge deep into her mouth, reveling as she curls her arms around my neck, slides her tongue along mine, and whimpers. I don't stop kissing her until she melts. Until she rubs against me. Until I own that mouth.

Jesus, I didn't expect to lose my fucking head, especially this fast...

Desperately sucking in air, I dig my fingers into her soft flesh, grinding my lips—and my cock—against her. I suck in her sweetness, inhaling her hint-of-coconut scent, hearing the little catches at the back of her throat, while staring at her closed eyes and rapt face. She consumes all my senses. I'm attuned to her. Only her. Always her? The way I feel now, I can't imagine getting enough of Skye. The lust she incites pounds me like a hurricane. I've never experienced anything quite like this. So, yeah, I'm going to need more.

How soon can I get her into bed?

Suddenly, Skye wrenches away, breathing heavily, and stares at me with the kind of gaping daze that says she's every bit as mowed down by our insane chemistry as I am. "I don't think we're going to have trouble convincing anyone we can't keep our hands off each other."

I just smile. "No, honey, we're not."

CHAPTER TWO

By Saturday evening, a couple of things have become exceedingly clear. First, Skye and I won't have trouble convincing anyone that I can't keep my hands off her because it's true. We've "practiced" our PDA almost nonstop for the last two days—until I'm sweating, hard, and mindless with hunger. I want Skye so fucking bad, but her body language says that, regardless of how much she's into me or how totally I arouse her, something holds her back from giving in.

Does she, deep down, have feelings for Finn?

Second, we know our cover story backward and forward. Thanks to two solid days of storms, she couldn't teach me to surf. Instead, we spent the time together, perfecting our act. We've even covered new ground— first jobs, first loves, schooling, dating, childhood pets, habits… We're prepared.

I pace the vacation rental, glad that I brought a suit, just in case. As I straighten my navy tie for the tenth time in as many minutes, she knocks and opens the front door. I turn to her—and stop in my tracks.

Skye takes my breath away.

Her hair is piled on top of her head in a 'do that's part braid and part bun with loose tendrils brushing her temples and nape. It's carefully arranged yet casual, a lot like her dress, which is a cheerful peach shade. A ruffle accents the front where she's loosened the top two buttons to reveal that lush cleavage I'm still dying to get my hands—and mouth—on. It gathers at the waist with a simple bow, emphasizing how tiny she is. To say the skirt ends at mid-thigh would be generous. The woman has great legs. No surprise she likes to show them off. Even if she doesn't belong to me, I wish she wasn't planning to flash them to a few dozen ogling bastards at this shindig.

"Wow. Are you trying to make Finn jealous?"

"He'll notice I brought you way before he notices how I look," she drawls as she scans me up and down. "But maybe you're hoping Dana will notice you?"

"Why would you think that?"

"You're a force to be reckoned with in that suit." She looks like she wants to touch me.

But she doesn't.

I hold out my hand. When she takes it, I'm gratified to see my ring on her finger, even if it's fake.

You need to slow your roll, man. Do you remember the meaning of the word pretend?

"Skye, we're supposed to be an engaged couple tonight. You can touch me any time."

"Yeah, the you in shorts and T-shirts. This you?" She gestures to my suit and bites her lip. "I wish we could go someplace else—just the two of us—and skip the wedding."

I totally wish that, too. "What if we did?"

Besides a night of mind-bending, blow-the-doors-off sex?

"Nothing would ever change for Dana and Finn. Plus, Sherry, his mother, would never forgive me. My own probably wouldn't, either."

I hold in a sigh of regret and lace our fingers together. "Then let's do this."

She presses a hand to her stomach. "I'll be a lot less nervous once tonight is over."

With a nod, I lead her outside and help her into my rental car. But the truth is, I'm reluctant for tomorrow. My business contact, David Chang, called while I was in the shower to inquire about the information I've gathered on the property. I've walked the beaches and explored the property lines. I've researched the zoning, infrastructure, and roads. This place would be great for development. A brand new, very private gem. Absolutely lucrative.

It sounds perfect…except Skye lives in the little unit up the hill. And she's worked here her whole adult life. There's a chance I'll be stripping both away by returning one call.

Then again, I have no idea if she's truly attached to this place. And Mr. Chang has only expressed interest. If I tell him this place is something he could develop, that doesn't mean he actually will. Even if he did, that could be years away. Still, I can't breathe a word of this to Skye. I'd be betraying the confidence of a valued client.

That's the truth...but I feel kind of guilty. And I don't like it. Personal relationships should never get in the way of business, especially since my profit from this deal could be north of five million dollars. Besides, everything between Skye and me is supposed to be fake, right? Yes, it feels awfully fucking real right now, but unless something changes between us I probably won't see her except in a professional capacity after this wedding.

And if tonight is the last chance I'll have to hold her, I intend to make the most of it.

The ride to the chapel is blessedly short. By mutual agreement, we arrive with ten minutes to spare, giving Finn's parents almost no time to do anything but give us a once-over from the front pew as an usher leads us to our seats.

Skye grips my hand tightly.

"Honey?"

"I'm fine."

As we sit, I lean close and drop my voice so no one else can hear. "Having second thoughts?"

"No." She tries to smile. "Not at all. Thank you for doing this, by the way."

I send her a grin to lighten the mood. "You can thank me with another sixty minutes on the massage table." *I also wouldn't turn down a night in my bed.*

She laughs, something light and real. Heads turn. Finn's mother glances over her shoulder at us again.

I lift Skye's hand to my mouth for a kiss, then turn it so she can see the sparkling engagement ring. "She's watching."

"I know."

"So let's play our parts. Come here." I tip a finger under Skye's chin.

Easily, naturally, she leans in and lays her plump pink lips over mine for a lingering second. I feel her trembling. When I cup her jaw, she seems to steady.

"We've got this," I promise her as I pull back, squeezing her shoulder.

She smiles and nods, then four men file in at the front of the chapel, positioning themselves near the altar.

"I'm guessing the guy in the black tux is Finn?"

The others are wearing gray.

"Yeah."

He's not what I expected. Medium height, medium build, medium brown hair. He looks perfectly...average. And completely fucking rattled.

When I catch him looking our way, I slide an arm around Skye's shoulders and pull her closer, acknowledging him with a lift of my chin.

He returns the gesture, then rubs his hands together, looking anxiously down the empty aisle. A string quartet plays soft music. His best man pats him on the back.

"Finn looks ready to puke. Think he's got cold feet?"

She shakes her head. "Crowds make him nervous. And the death-glare I'm sure his mother is giving him probably isn't helping."

"You're one-hundred-percent sure you don't still have feelings for him?"

"One-thousand percent. Trust me. Dana is his other half, and I just want him to be happy."

I've spent enough time studying Skye now to know she means that.

"Good." I kiss her again, mostly because I can't resist.

Then the music changes. Bridesmaids glide up the center of the chapel, dressed in black dresses with a purple lacy overlay. The result looks like something out of a Tim Burton movie. Now that I think about it, everything does, especially the black tapers burning at the altar.

When the three attendants, all carrying bouquets of purple and white roses with black baby's breath, stop at the end of the aisle and turn to the small crowd, I murmur in Skye's ear, "Is this a goth wedding?"

"Uh-huh."

"Because Dana is a goth girl?" She must be. Finn looks way too country club to have thought of this motif.

Skye doesn't have time to answer me before the music changes once more. I recognize the tune the string quartet is playing as Evanescence's "My Immortal." Then, at the back of the chapel, the bride appears. She's wearing traditional white—with black velvet embellishments on the strapless bodice and figure-hugging skirt. A sheer black veil covers her face, sweeping all the way down to her toes in front and brushing the chapel's black runner behind her.

Whoa.

Most of the ceremony passes in a blur. It's thankfully short, but I feel Skye tense every time Finn's mother turns to give her an imploring stare. Does the woman think she's going to stand up and object?

Finally, the officiant instructs the groom to kiss the bride, and he lifts the veil over her head. A few gasps from the attendees are quickly smothered, but that doesn't lessen the surprise of the bride's unexpected cherry red hair, the giant red tattoo of a phoenix that covers her chest, or her pitch-black lipstick.

It's their wedding, so whatever makes them happy is what their ceremony should be. Skye doesn't seem to think it's out of the ordinary. She's smiling, likely because Finn looks so damn happy as he lays a big one on his bride's lips and they're officially pronounced man and wife. But Finn's mother is clearly less than thrilled with her out-of-the-norm daughter-in-law. I don't know Dana, but I feel sorry for her.

When Finn and his wife run out of the chapel, hands clasped high in the air, the attendants follow. Then the guests start filing out. Skye and I rise.

The reception is in the adjacent building. As we enter, music blasts. The bride and groom already have drinks in hand. And the party is getting underway.

Then Finn's mother approaches.

"Skye, you look lovely." The woman kisses her cheek.

"Thanks, Sherry." She introduces me, and as I shake the older woman's hand, Skye chats nervously. "The wedding was touching."

The woman sighs. "I did the best I could. Dana really didn't want my input." Then she turns her speculative gaze on me. "So tell me about your new boyfriend. You haven't been together long, right?"

"Fiancé," I correct. "We've been together long enough to know we're perfect for each other. I can't wait to marry this girl."

By my side, Skye squeezes my hand in thanks. "It's been quick...but when you know, you know."

Sherry stiffens. "That's what Finn said, but I think it's important that couples truly learn each other inside and out. They should know each other the way you and Finn do before they commit themselves."

Well, there's a nice subversive little dig.

When I see Skye's deer-in-the-headlights expression, I step in. "And sometimes long-term dating is more an indication that people are simply comfortable in a relationship, rather than madly in love. These last few months have been the happiest of my life. I didn't expect to meet this woman." I bring Skye closer and press a kiss to her temple. "But now I can't imagine my life without her."

"Are you moving here, Stephen?"

We discussed this part of our cover story, too. "No. I have to go back to New York in a few weeks. The real world calls… I'm taking Skye with me, so she can experience the life and pace there. Eventually, she'll acclimate."

If Sherry thinks for a while that Skye will be out of reach, even better.

"Good luck. She'll hate it there." Sherry smiles tightly, then turns to Skye before I can respond. "So have your parents met Stephen yet? It seems odd they didn't call to tell me about him. Or tell me that you're engaged."

"I-I talked to Mom yesterday," Skye falters, then gets it together. "She knew you'd been busy and figured you'd meet Stephen today anyway. I can't wait to introduce him to my folks."

"Oh?" Sherry perks up, like she thinks there's hope since I haven't met Mr. and Mrs. Ingram. "When will that be?"

"Soon," I tell the woman as I drop another kiss on my "fiancée's" temple. "I'm looking forward to meeting Jennifer and Sam."

"And they're looking forward to meeting him," Skye puts in more confidently.

"I'm sure." Sherry turns to me, eyes watering. "This girl is very special. But you know that."

"Yes, ma'am, I do."

Skye plays her part by smiling up at me adoringly. I can't not stare at her. I can't stop myself from getting lost in her eyes. I can't not kiss her.

When I bend to take her lips, she meets me halfway, clinging softly to me. As I do every time I touch her, I get caught up in her scent, the subtle changes in her body that tell me I affect her, the feel of her against me. I know the moment she stops worrying about Sherry and focuses on us. It's so fucking heady it takes all of my restraint not to leave the reception to take her home—and kiss her straight into bed.

Yeah, our act is supposed to be fake…but what I'm feeling is getting realer by the moment.

For my own sanity, I pull back and smile Sherry's way. I'm a little startled to see the man I assume is her husband standing beside her. He introduces himself as Russell, grazes his lips across Skye's cheek, then tells his wife that the caterer has questions.

I'm relieved when the pair disappears. "That went pretty well."

Skye nods. "I think she believes us, at least so far."

"She does and we won't give her any reason to change her mind. We can do this for another three hours."

"You're right."

A passing waiter saunters by with a tray of bubbly. I snag two and hand one to Skye. "To an enjoyable and successful night."

That earns me a smile. "Absolutely."

After the champagne, the buffet opens. We grab plates and sit at a table with some of Finn and Skye's high school friends. I'm expecting a grilling, but they're all too busy posting on social media and chatting amongst themselves to do more than ask a few cursory questions.

After dinner, the deejay starts spinning tunes. The father-daughter dance is touching, and it's clear to see the plumber from Cleveland is both happy and sad that his little girl is now another man's wife. Dana looks equally moved by these moments with her father, and she tries furiously to stop her mascara from running.

The mother-son dance follows. By comparison, it's silent, almost stiff. Displeasure rolls off Sherry, and every time she looks Skye's way, I make sure I'm touching her. I don't want to give Finn's mother any reason to keep making Skye feel wretchedly guilty for not being in love with her son.

When it's over, the parents of the bride and groom are invited to dance to a tune from some rat-pack crooner. Finn takes that opportunity to grab his wife's hand and lead her in our direction.

I stand and help Skye to her feet, meeting the newly married couple halfway, near an empty corner of the room.

"Hi, guys. Congratulations." Skye hugs Finn, then Dana. "You look beautiful."

The goth girl perks up. "Thanks."

"Doesn't she?" Finn holds her close. "I feel so lucky."

Dana elbows him, but her smile says she's pleased. "You look great, Skye."

With the niceties out of the way, the gazes of both bride and groom fall on me.

I turn on a smile and hold out my hand. "Stephen."

The other guy shakes it. "Finn. My wife—gosh, it sounds amazing to say that—Dana."

"Thanks for coming." The goth girl smiles my way, obviously meaning it.

I send her a congratulatory grin. "It's my pleasure."

Dana turns back to Skye. "Can you spare a minute?"

Skye blinks up at me, looking as surprised as I feel, then she shrugs. "Sure."

"I'd appreciate some advice," Dana explains as she leads Skye to a quiet spot a few feet away, and the two begin talking.

I can't tell what they're discussing, but Dana looks both earnest and scared. Skye holds the bride's hands in reassurance. She's got a big heart. What would it be like if I could have even a little corner of it?

"So where did Skye find you?" Finn narrows his eyes as he drops his voice. "Oh, fuck. Tell me you're not an escort."

Is he for real?

"No."

"An actor?"

"No. Why does it matter where she 'found' me? She did this for you, and things are going well."

"Yeah. Totally. And my mom is buying it, which is great. I just wanted to make sure you know you're only in Skye's life temporarily. The way you're touching her makes me wonder if you forgot."

Why the hell would he give a shit? "Come again?"

"Seriously, brah, you're a smooth guy, probably a player. We both know you're not staying. I'm sure you've guessed Skye is a little naive...and I see the way she looks at you."

"Looks at me?"

"Like she's got a sweet tooth, and you're the meltiest bar of chocolate she's ever laid eyes on. That's great for this event. And I agree that she needs to meet someone she's actually attracted to—eventually. But she's the kind of girl who doesn't get physical unless she's really, truly attached. I don't want you hurting her just because she was nice enough to do me a solid."

There are so many things wrong with what he just said. "You think I'm doing her this favor because I'm hoping she'll give me a piece of ass?"

Finn hesitates as if he realizes he insulted me. "Look, I don't mean anything by it. I just—"

"No, you look. I work in international acquisitions and investments.

I'm not a gigolo or a hack. And don't ever intimate that I'm the kind of asshole who would expect to use her because I let her use me."

He holds up two hands. "Okay. I got it. Sorry. I just needed to know what's up."

I don't owe Finn an explanation. What Skye and I have is between us. "It's under control."

His nod tells me he doesn't like my answer, but he backs off. "Okay. Have you thought about how you'll stage your breakup?"

Skye asked me a couple of days ago, and I put off answering. In truth, I've avoided thinking about it. And the more time that passes...the less I want to.

"Dude, didn't you just get married? Don't you have your own life to focus on?"

Finn grinds his teeth. "Skye is my friend."

"Who is smart enough to make her own decisions," I counter. "So far I don't see you being any less nosy than your mom."

That makes Finn reel back. "For real?"

"Is Skye up in your business about your relationship with Dana?"

"We don't need help."

"We don't, either."

He drops his voice. "We both know this is all a show, and you're going to leave her sooner rather than later."

"Do we? Did it ever occur to you that maybe I'm doing this because I'm having feelings for Skye?"

Finn looks stunned. "Whoa. I didn't see that coming."

"That makes two of us."

At that, he smiles and claps me on the shoulder. "It happens, man. I didn't expect to fall for Dana after we hooked up...but here we are."

I give him a vague smile as I glance over his head to watch the two women. Dana dabs at her eyes again, then hugs Skye, who embraces her in return. Then they head our way and put a merciful end to our tête-à-tête.

After the four of us exchange some stilted chitchat, the deejay invites everyone to dance. The newly married couple takes that as their cue to return to the head table.

I lead Skye to our seats. "You okay? What did Dana want?"

"Advice on getting Sherry to like her. I feel bad... Her new mother-in-law hates everything she loves—tattoos, loud music, her bright hair.

Frankly, I think those are all things Finn loves about Dana, too. But Sherry wants someone 'normal' who will fit in at the country club, so..."

"What did you tell her?"

"To be herself. Sherry is either going to come around or not, but it's more important for her to stay true to herself than to try to be someone she isn't. She'll only be miserable."

Yes. Like Skye, Dana seems to have a strong sense of self. I applaud that.

Especially since I'm struggling to understand who I am without my job. I always thought I'd be the next CEO of Colossus; I've been groomed for the position my whole life. I've wanted it as long as I can remember. I've given up so much socially and personally to prove to my dad that I'm worthy of the role. In return, he only proved to me that the worship I've had for him since I was a kid was misplaced.

Where does that leave me?

I manage to dig out of my maudlin thoughts and smile. "Good advice."

"What did Finn say?"

Besides demonstrating that, if he wants to, he could be a pain in my ass? "Nothing important."

I see the question on Skye's face, but before she can ask it, Sherry turns from her place on the dance floor to dissect my interaction with Skye.

My girl looks nervous again, so I stand and pull her to her feet. "Let's dance."

"I'm not very good at it."

"Lucky for you I am. Lots of practice, thanks to cotillion and all Mom's soirées while I was growing up." I wink.

"Thank you for trying to make tonight enjoyable. I've been dreading it."

"I don't blame you." I tap her nose. "But I'm determined to make sure you have a good time." And people are more likely to believe we're a couple if we seem not to have a care in the world.

We bop our way through a Black-Eyed Peas' party song and get a little cheeky when Walk the Moon echoes what I'm thinking with "Shut Up and Dance." Then the deejay slows things down a little with Stevie Wonder's "Isn't She Lovely?"

"You really can dance." Skye sounds surprised. "You actually make me look halfway decent."

"You're doing great. Are you having a good time now?"

"Yeah." She flashes me the first genuine smile I've seen all day. "Thanks."

"You keep thanking me. You don't have to."

"Without you, I would have come to this thing alone, and Sherry would have been all over me."

The woman would have browbeat her, and Skye is too polite to tell her to shove it up her ass and let her son live his own life.

The song changes again, and Bruno Mars croons, "I think I wanna marry you…"

I can't resist stroking her cheek. "I'm happy we're here together."

But what will happen when this wedding is over? When I have to return Mr. Chang's call? When I decide my future and leave the island, probably for good? If I want to test the possibility there's something lasting between us, I have to make a move. Otherwise, Skye will always think I'm acting.

"I'm happy we're here together, too." Her words are soft and heartfelt.

So I swallow—and go for broke. "Have you figured out yet that I'm genuinely interested in you?"

Her startled gaze jerks up to meet my stare. "It's not a show?"

"Honey, I'm a good liar…but not that good. I was interested the minute I saw you in my living room fluffing pillows and talking on the phone."

"Really?"

I don't know why she's shocked. "Really. You're beautiful and sweet and funny. You care about the feelings of the people around you. It would have been perfectly normal for you to want my help so you wouldn't have to deal with Sherry anymore. Instead, you were more concerned about Finn and his parents accepting Dana into their family. Where I come from, people are always looking to extract something from others— power, money, access, knowledge—you name it. You're going way out of your way just to help a friend."

"So…you didn't agree to be my fiancé for the night for the massages?"

"No. They're damn nice, and I'll take them, but…"

"And you didn't do it to avoid dealing with your own problems?"

"It started that way, but every moment I've spent with you since has been about you. Only you. What I'm feeling is real. I want you way more than I want to fool the people around us. I want you tonight, tomorrow…" I hold her closer, stare into her wide brown eyes. "I want to see about the future."

And there's Bruno Mars again, singing about getting married.

"Please tell me you want that, too," I whisper.

Her fingers tighten on my shoulders as she seems to fall deep into my gaze. "I do."

Thank fuck. "Good. Are we done here? Can I take you home now?"

"Please," she whispers.

I swoop down for a kiss, ply her lips with passion, before I force myself to pull back. "Can I take you to bed? Make love to you?"

She bites her lip.

"Honey?"

She swallows. Her answer turns even breathier. "Yes."

* * * *

The drive that had seemed so short when we headed to the chapel now takes a million damn years. With Skye's hand tucked in mine, I navigate the slick roads through another evening rain shower. The car is too silent. I have no idea what she's thinking. Is she reconsidering? Wishing she hadn't impulsively agreed to spend the night with me?

When we arrive back at Aloha Rainbow house, I pull the sedan under the carport, then dash around to open her door. Skye steps out, her big, dark eyes gleaming up at me in the moonlight. It's obvious she has something heavy on her mind.

As the wind starts to howl and the surprisingly cool rain blows in to splatter us, I slide my hand across the small of her back, shelter her from the elements with my body, and guide her inside.

If she halts our night together, I wouldn't blame her. We haven't known each other for long, and from what Finn said flings aren't her thing. She doesn't know about my interest in this property. Or how seriously I'm starting to feel about her. She's a girl who leads with her heart, and my fucked-up life probably makes me look like a bad decision.

Closing the door behind us, I turn to her in the entryway. "Skye, honey, I—"

"Are you changing your mind?"

"No." Is she insane? "Absolutely not. But—"

"Thank god."

With a sigh of relief, she kicks off her boho beaded wedges, tosses aside her purse, and plasters herself against me, pressing her lips to mine.

I'm all too happy to open up and kiss her. I've hooked up more than my fair share, but I don't remember ever deriving such singular pleasure from simply kissing a woman. There's something about Skye… She's sweet but slightly exotic. The way she fills my mouth boldly one moment, then retreats coyly the next makes me so hot.

She pulls back, panting. "You're sure?"

"Honey, the only thing that will keep me off you tonight is if you say no."

"When it comes to you, I'm afraid I don't know that word."

Is she feeling this insane desire, too? The same inexplicable gut-sense of rightness and inevitability, like we met because the stars aligned and this was meant to be? It sounds hokey, and I've never believed in any power beyond one's own intelligence and good planning. But I didn't scheme this seduction at all, and my feelings aren't logical. None of that changes how much I need to touch this woman.

"Good." I lift her into my arms, cradling her against my chest. "Put your arms around my neck."

Instantly, she complies, and I start up the stairs. By the time I reach the top and flip the switch to turn on the bedside lamp, I'm breathing heavily, and it's not just the physical exertion that has my body going haywire. Anticipation, thick and ripe, hangs in the air. I have this sense that whatever happens next will change everything.

When I cross the threshold to the bedroom, I set her on her feet, slowly brushing her body against mine. Without her heels, she barely reaches my shoulders, but that doesn't stop her from cupping my nape, pulling my mouth down to hers, and opening beneath me.

I sink into her and lose myself in everything that makes Skye uniquely her. Frantically, I tug on the pins that keep her silken hair from spilling into my hands. She nudges my fingers aside, then quickly dismantles her 'do and gives her tresses a wild shake before she attacks my suit coat and tears it from my shoulders.

As she tosses it on a nearby chair, I kick out of my shoes and lay into the buttons down my chest, slipping them free one after the other, and yanking the tails from my pants until my shirt hangs open.

"I want to touch you…" she murmurs.

The second her fingertips skate up my abs and across my chest, I shudder. "You've massaged me for sixty minutes every day since we've met. It's my turn to touch you."

She sends me a breathless little smile. "That's an unfair comparison. I tried to look at you academically."

"Did you succeed?"

A pink flush crawls up her cheeks. "Notice I said tried."

"So that's a no." I grin. "For the record, I've never looked at you as anything other than a woman. I'm dying to get my hands on you."

Her eyes slide shut. "When you say things like that, it makes me flash hot everywhere."

"Oh, honey… If you like what I'm saying, wait until you feel what I can do for you."

"I don't want to wait. Hurry."

"On it." I shrug my dress shirt onto the floor, not giving a shit if it wrinkles.

Her eyes widen and she consumes me with a greedy stare as I untie the bow at her waist and put my fingers to work unfastening the little buttons down the front of her dress.

It seems to take endless patience, but soon the ruffles lie askew. I see the lace of her ivory underwire bra. The pretty pink of her puckered nipples are a shadow beneath. I'm desperate to thumb them, pinch them, suck them, spank them. God, how pretty would they be pierced? The thought makes me unbearably hard.

I want her naked, not just physically. I need her emotionally bare for me. Once she is, I have a feeling she'll be everything—and more—I've fantasized about for four seemingly endless days.

"Stephen, do something besides stare at me."

"I will. Right now, I'm trying to decide how not to scare the hell out of you."

"Scare me?"

"You don't understand the way I want you…"

A little smile flits across her face. "Show me."

There's no stopping this. I don't want to. Apparently, neither does she.

"Any other fastenings or hooks on this dress?"

"No."

"If I rip it, will it be the end of the world?"

"No." Her voice shakes. She bites her lip.

My restraint is toast.

I yank the belt from her waist and toss it aside. Then I tug the short, peachy dress over her head and fling it to the other side of the room. She stands in front of me wearing so little, it can barely be called lingerie. I swallow my tongue as I trace the edge of the scalloped, low-cut lace cradling her breast, dangerously close to her nipple. But the tiny panties with a peekaboo keyhole above her pussy turns the heat up on the blaze inside me until it's close to an inferno.

"Holy fuck," I breathe.

"Do you like it?"

"Like isn't the right word." I lust. I hunger. I covet. I need.

"I bought it this morning, hoping..." She swallows. "You know."

I file that interesting factoid away. "I've been hoping, too."

But I don't know precisely what it means to touch her. I don't know what it means to be inside her, getting lost in her, feeling ecstasy with her, giving her the kind of pleasure that makes her whimper and scream. And I don't know what it means to have her love, to hold her heart in my hand, to call her mine.

And I can't fucking explain why—it makes no sense—but I want to know.

"Stephen?" She looks nervous. She's probably wondering why I still haven't pounced on her. Or is that her impatience talking?

I smile as I circle behind her, trailing my fingertips across the swells of her breasts before I pause, pressing myself against her back and settling my lips at her ear. "You feel the anticipation?"

She nods.

"Does it make your blood sing?"

"I've never felt anything like this."

"How long have your nipples been hard?"

"Most of the night."

I slip an arm around her waist and dip my hands between her legs. The lace covering her pussy is more than damp. "You're wet."

"You do that to me," she moans.

Her answer makes me smile. "Tonight isn't the first time?"

"No. Stephen..." She juts her hips forward, pressing in to my touch.

"I'm not rushing, honey. We've got all night." When she whimpers, I circle my fingers over the wet fabric right where she's sensitive. "And I've been hard for you for days."

She reaches back and digs her fingernails into my thigh. "Why are we still waiting?"

Normally, I would torment her a little longer because her wanting me is so delicious. But her impatience is destructive to my self-control.

I reach for the hooks of her bra and unfasten them before letting the flimsy contraption fall at her feet.

In the next moment, I hear a mechanical click as the air conditioner kicks on. Cool air blows from the overhead vents. As I hover over her shoulder, I skim the side of her breast with my knuckles—and see her nipples draw up even tighter.

She shivers. Her breathing turns choppy.

"If you haven't been kissed properly in two years, how long has it been since you've had sex?"

Skye turns in my arms and unbuttons my slacks with one hand. The other she curls over my zipper, around my hard cock, giving me a squeeze that makes me hiss. "Stop talking and get your pants off."

Maybe I should push harder to make her answer me, but I'm done putting off what we both want.

I practically yank out my zipper in my haste to get it down, then shove my pants around my ankles. Now we're both standing, bodies pressed together, wearing only our underwear and our naked desire. I want to kiss her, make sure she knows this is special. Instead, my desperation does the talking. I lift her off the floor, roll her onto the mattress, and settle on top of her, spreading her thighs with my insistent legs and notching my aching cock against the softest, wettest part of her.

Instantly, she cries out and digs her fingers into my back. I'm ready to get inside her—then something awful occurs to me.

"I don't have any condoms."

She winces in the shadowy room, an apology filling her dark eyes. "I should have thought about that."

No, I should have, but I didn't want to assume. "Tell me you're on the pill."

"I haven't had a reason to be."

Fuck. "I'll go to the store."

"It should be fine."

"Should be?"

"I finished my period three days ago."

It's not a perfect solution. Hell, it's not even a good one. But the math seems all right, and I'm too fucking needy to wait. "I'm clean, but are you sure?"

"Yes. I can't stand not having you inside me. I feel like I've been waiting for you my whole life."

I met this woman mere days ago, and in a weird way, I feel as if I've been waiting for her my whole life, too.

"Be really sure. Once I start…"

"I won't ask you to stop. I want you too much."

Everything she says pours gasoline on my raging fire. I hope like hell she doesn't regret tonight, but I already know that, no matter what happens, I won't.

"I've never wanted any woman the way I want you, Skye. Kiss me."

A shy smile spreads across her face before she lifts her head and slants her lips across mine. In less than two seconds, she's inside my mouth and my raging desire takes over.

I kiss my way down her neck, dragging my lips over her stunningly soft skin, stopping to savor her, inhale her, as I inch closer and closer to her irresistible pink peaks. She arches, encouraging me. I cup her breast. It fits perfectly in my palm as I bend and take her nipple in my mouth.

She seems to melt on my tongue, writhing, clutching, moaning. Sucking on her is a delight. I treat the other to the same handling, squeezing the first between my thumb and fingers.

Nothing about Skye is jaded or been-there-done-that. She's so sensitive, so responsive. I could lap at her all day, and at some point I will. Tonight, I have to possess every part of her. I have to put my stamp on her. I have to give her at least a few orgasmic reasons not to wake up tomorrow and convince herself that these past few days have been anything less than real.

I journey my way down her body, skimming the long expanse of her stomach, lips grazing the lean curve of her waist. I wend down further, pulling her delicate, sexy-as-fuck panties past her thighs, then over her knees, before chucking them across the room.

"I'll never find all my clothes."

"You're not going to need them until morning. And maybe not even then."

She smiles, looking somewhere between amused and aroused—until I wrap my hands around her thighs, spread them wide, and wedge my shoulders between them.

"Stephen?" she breathes, wide-eyed.

"Skye." I steady her by petting her—sleek legs, lush hips, pouting pussy.

"Are you really going to…" She wriggles under me, unconsciously giving me better access to her slick, silken folds.

"Taste you? Tongue-fuck you? Make you come? Yes."

She drags in a shuddering breath. Her eyes darken. I smell her in the air. Yeah, she wants this. God knows I do…

I part her with my thumbs and bend, dragging in her scent as I stroke my tongue through her wet folds.

Jesus, she's so soft. And addicting. Her tangy-sweet flavor itself is a tease, so light I find myself lapping up all I can get, then chasing down more at the source. But no matter how many times I circle her swollen clit or burrow my tongue inside her, I can't seem to get enough.

Soon, she's panting under me, keening, her body pitching. In the spill of golden light from the lamp, I see perspiration sheen her torso. Her plump nipples stab the air. The power that pumps through me at knowing I can lavish her with pleasure yanks at the chain of my restraint.

I want to see her squirm. I want to hear her beg. I want to feel her all around me.

As her needy bud swells between my lips and I insert a pair of fingers in her tight-as-fuck opening, she cries out.

"You want to come, honey?"

Skye nods fervently. "Yes." She curls her hands around the sheets and tugs, breath seesawing, hips undulating. "Please…"

"Tell me."

"I want to come," she gasps.

I usually enjoy the push-pull that leads to a woman's inevitable surrender every bit as much as I enjoy her surrender itself. But this is different. Skye is different. Every part of me aches for her to cede herself, trust me with her body and place her soul in my hands, give me her heart.

Eagerly, I lick her distended clit before sucking it into my mouth, then probe the smooth spot inside her with my searching fingers.

"Stephen!" she cries out as her body tenses.

Her legs straighten. Her audible breaths turn labored before her respiration stutters. Her eyes widen, then slam shut. Color runs through her body, settling pink in her cheeks, her chest, and the swollen folds of her pussy.

Fuck yes.

Then she lets loose a throaty wail of bliss.

I feel her clamp on my fingers, pulsing as she bucks and scratches for more. I give it to her, steeped in a soul-deep gratification as I string out her trembling pleasure for long, shocking moments until she finally turns into a shuddering, panting puddle.

While she catches her breath, I climb my way up her body, pressing kisses across her skin before taking her mouth and spreading her tempting essence across her tongue. I drink in her passion, delighting in how shaken she is by the ecstasy.

"Stephen…" she whispers.

I see the question in her eyes. What the hell just happened? How much longer before I'll be inside her? How much more pleasure will I wring from her before the night is over? How much of her soul will I take?

She may not want the truth.

Beneath me, I spread her pliant body and nestle between her thighs, positioning myself in between and aligning my aching crest with her slick opening. Just the feel of her flesh grasping for my sensitive head has me eager to push in, plunge deep, and take total possession.

I manage to hold back. "Last chance, honey. If you want to back out…"

"No!" She wraps her legs around my waist, bringing me closer, holding me tighter. "I want you inside me."

"Thank god." I grit my teeth and grip her hips. "I need you so fucking bad."

With a groan, I start pushing my way in. Skye is slick and hot, but so damn tight. I ease back, then stroke in a little deeper. But she's clutched closed against me, no matter how I press or cajole.

Frustration gnaws at me.

I dig for patience, pull back, and thumb her clit in slow, gentle circles. "Relax, honey."

"I am. Well, I'm trying."

She is. The rest of her body seems loose, almost boneless. I have a sneaking suspicion why she's so tight.

"Seriously, how long has it been?"

She glances away. "Please just try again."

I cup her chin and bring her gaze back. "I'm not grilling you, just wanting to give you the best experience possible. How long?"

"Promise you won't laugh."

"I would never laugh at you."

Skye licks her lips. "I haven't had sex since I was sixteen."

Oh, fuck.

She's twenty-four now. From our conversations, I know she hasn't dated a lot. School activities, strict parents, and other shit ensured she kept her head down. But I never imagined that equated to eight fucking years of celibacy.

I probably should have. For all her offbeat-colored toe polish and bohemian dresses, she's shy. And Finn told me straight up she isn't the kind of girl who gives her body easily. I have to hope she's with me tonight because this means something to her.

"Drake was my first real boyfriend. It only lasted a few months."

Reading between the lines, what she means is that their relationship was rocky and angst-filled and she was gun-shy about giving romance another try.

Until me.

I cup her face and kiss her mouth. "It's okay. I'll do whatever you need. I'll slow down. I'll be gentle. I'll—"

"Don't you dare. Every time I fantasized about us, I imagined you taking me and not holding anything back."

I imagined that, too. I lay in bed and dreamed about it. I showered and masturbated to thoughts of it. No way I can't give her what we're both aching for.

"I will. I promise. Right now, just kiss me."

She does, her shyness melting away as she shows me the woman underneath, revealing both her open acceptance and a quiet desperation—neither of which I can resist. What's even sexier? Just like I've learned how she feels and what she responds to, she's also figuring me out. She seems to have noticed that I moan when she digs her fingers into my back. And that when she rakes her nails across my scalp, I shudder. And she's clearly clued in that I love it when she drags her tongue up my neck and nips at my lobe.

But I can't let her undo me yet. So I grab her hands, lace our fingers together, and hold them against the mattress before I take her lips in a blistering kiss. I feel my ring on her finger. Even if it's fake, knowing it's there does something really real to me.

Slowly, she gives way under me. I focus on sinking into her mouth, on melding our skin. Beneath me, she syncs up to the rhythm I set with the stroke of my tongue, the purse of my lips, the sound of my rough inhalation before we do it all again.

I'm completely lost in Skye when I fit my throbbing cock against her opening again. This time, I slide slow and deep with almost no resistance, not stopping until I reach the hilt.

She gasps into our kiss. I fucking moan. She's perfect. Hot, smooth, tight…all of that—but more. And I'm taking her bareback. It's stupid. It's dangerous. I've managed to make it to the ripe age of thirty-two without ever going in gloveless. But Skye isn't the kind of woman who would get pregnant intentionally for access to my fortune. I've never simply trusted any other woman I've shared sheets with. Or maybe my desire is talking and I'm letting the wrong head make my decisions.

But I don't think so.

"Oh, fuck," I growl in her ear, rooting as deep as I can because I never want to leave this snug heaven. "Honey…"

"This is…"—she breathes with what sounds like sublime pleasure—"nothing like I remember. This is everything."

If she was sixteen, he was probably the same age. High school sex is pretty much the blind leading the blind. If I can't surpass that benchmark as a grown-ass man, I don't have any business touching her.

"Absolutely everything," I second as I cradle her face in my hands, fuse our lips together again, and unleash all the pent-up need I've held in for days.

I fuck her slow and strong, letting every bit of her feel every inch of me as I settle into an unhurried rhythm, every thrust punctuated with a groan from me and a gasp from her. We're so in tune, I can feel her desire climbing. I know the moment her body overtakes her mind and instinct pushes her beyond all thought except the coming pleasure.

"Stephen…" Her nails dig into me more.

Hunger claws me deeper, becoming a craving I'm not sure I'll ever shake.

"You going to come with me inside you?"

"I-I think so. I've never…"

Of course she hasn't, and the idea that I'll be the one to show her so many delicious firsts juices up the passion in my bloodstream even more. The stirrings of climax tickle my spine, tingle in my balls. Oh, yeah. This is going to be mammoth.

But I need to immerse Skye in undeniable, inescapable pleasure first. I need to deliver some shock and awe. I need to addict her so that when she wakes up tomorrow she can't imagine walking away from me.

Digging my knees into the mattress, I curl my fingers deeper into her hips and lift her a fraction. I use my whole body to thrust in. The bed shakes. I slide deeper. She lets loose a high-pitched wail that only gets louder each time I work my way into her.

Her clutching fingers bend until I feel her nails curl desperately into my shoulders. I welcome the sting of pain. It boils my blood. It spurs me to ride her harder and faster.

I surge into her with all my might, drag my crest against her sensitive spots, and revel in her tensing beneath me. "Come. I feel you. I need it."

"Stephen…" she shrieks.

"Yes." I bare my teeth in a growl. "Give in. Give it to me."

Beneath me, she's restless and writhing, heels buried in the mattress as she lifts to meet my every shove through the clamp of her cunt. My labored breath seesaws as I see the pink flush of her cheeks turn red. Her eyes slam shut. Her body freezes.

"Yes!" I thrust in. "That's it…"

Skye comes apart for me, shattering and shuddering in a throaty scream that vibrates down my spine, cuts the lifeline on my remaining restraint, and sends me plowing into her mercilessly.

I should pull out, but the ecstasy barrages me before I can do anything more than press into her as far as I can and let go with a shout of shocked pleasure.

The heart-roaring, tingling squall of climax is endless and perfect. Stupefying. Life-altering.

I belong here. I'm determined to do whatever I have to in order to stay here, make her mine every day, every night, every time I'm hungry. Any time she needs me.

I'm her man.

Despite the fact it's a really lousy time, I think I might just have fallen in love.

CHAPTER THREE

When the orgasm—and my realization—release their hold on me, I drag in a gasping breath and grapple with a whole bunch of *oh-holy-shit-what-just-happened?*

Skye falls back to the bed panting and limp and wearing an adorable Mona-Lisa smile of satisfaction. "Wow."

"Uh-huh." It's all I can manage now.

"Things have changed since I was sixteen."

Things have changed for me since my last hookup—and that was only three days before I flew out here. But what's really different? My circumstance? Not relevant. My attitude? Not really. My lover? Absolutely.

Skye makes all the difference.

"If you want to test that again—you know, to be really sure—give me a few minutes." I reluctantly withdraw from her and grab tissues from the nearby nightstand, giving us both a quick clean up. But there's something so satisfyingly primal about smelling my semen on her. "I promise I'll be ready."

"Are you kidding? I'm still catching my breath." She presses a hand to her chest. "Clearly, you've had a lot more practice at this than I have."

"I have." I'm not going to lie. "But tonight is special. You're special."

"Really?" The way her big, dark eyes take me in I can tell she wants to believe me and she's not sure she should.

"Really. No joke, just honesty. I'll always do my best to give that to you."

Under me, she smiles as if my words have reassured her and cups my cheek. "You're not at all who I thought you were when I first met you."

"Oh?" I raise a brow at her.

"You seemed New York slick, and I didn't see how I could possibly trust you…but you've done exactly what you promised. You learned me enough to convince Sherry that we're a couple. And you dropped everything to do it. Finn and Dana have some breathing room to enjoy married life. You've been wonderful. And you've made me feel special."

I stroke the damp tendrils from her face. "I'll let you in on a secret. I didn't learn you to fool your ex's mom. I did it because I wanted to. I meant what I said at the wedding; it wasn't a line to get you into bed. I'm genuinely interested in you."

The way her mouth curls up tells me that makes her happy. "I'm really interested in you, too." Then her smile falters. "But you're only here temporarily—"

"A month." I rented Aloha Rainbow house for a long while to make sure I got time and perspective. Since it's a hugely important decision, I need to be sure.

But after tonight, I'm pretty sure Skye will have some sway on my choice. At the moment, I can't imagine life without her. I don't know what being with her more permanently will look like yet, but I know I want her.

"That's a long time for a vacation, but not enough to know—"

"It's not just a vacation, honey."

She nods. "I know you're deciding your future because you and your dad disagree about your half-sister."

"Yeah."

"Want to talk about it?"

"Not really, but the issue isn't going to go away." I sigh. "You sure you want to hear all this? It's a lot."

"If it affects you, yes. I don't know that I can help, but I'm willing to listen."

If I'm going to make Skye a part of my life, she should know what's happening. It's only fair to let her decide if my shit is too much for her to handle.

"Thanks." I search for my courage. Now it gets difficult. "I knew Dad wasn't happy with my mother when I was growing up. She suffered from depression and seemed bitter about everything. My dad was ambitious and always hustling to put together deals, so he wasn't around much. I won't deny that he was a workaholic, which depressed my mom more. And the more depressed she got, the more bitterly she behaved…so the more he worked. It was a vicious cycle. I found out early that I'd rather be at the office with him than walking on eggshells at home with Mom."

"I'm so sorry to hear that. My parents were great. My childhood was idyllic. I count myself really lucky."

That's probably why Skye has such a big heart; it's never truly been crushed. I feel compelled to make sure no one ever does.

Another reason I should be as honest as I can.

"Not me." I had all the money in the world, but I learned early that, while it could buy material possessions, it couldn't buy love. "I was about seven when I figured out my parents lived together but weren't really together. I spent the night at a friend's house and noticed that his mom and dad didn't have separate bedrooms. Not long after, I saw our maid, Jina, follow my dad into his bedroom. Then he shut the door. Neither came out for hours."

Her eyes widen. "They were having an affair?"

"Definitely."

"Did your mom know?"

"At the time?" I shrug. "We never talked about it. But Jina left abruptly one day. I never saw her again. When I was a teenager, my dad got drunk one night and admitted that he and my mom had gotten pregnant with my sister, Amanda, to try to save their marriage. He knew almost right away it wouldn't work, but he couldn't afford to divorce her. Shortly after that, he started an affair with our maid…who also got pregnant. Mom found out and threatened to bleed him dry in divorce court, so he fired Jina, gave her a financial settlement for the child, and refused to have anything to do with either of them."

"Oh, my gosh. That's horrible."

I nod. "After dad told me about Nia, I was always curious. All I had was a bit of basic information about her, but out there somewhere was a sister I didn't know. So imagine my surprise when I dropped in to see a business contact in Seattle and realized his assistant was the very sister I'd never met."

"Oh, wow. Did she know you were her brother?"

"No clue. I wanted to get to know her. Since my mom had passed away a few years prior, I assumed my dad would, too. He didn't."

"And you were shocked."

"Yeah. Hugely."

"Do you have any idea why he doesn't want anything to do with her?"

"None. He's made a million excuses for Amanda, even though she's screwed up a hundred times. He even supported her when she got pregnant by his best friend."

"Your dad's best friend? How old is this man?"

"Was. Barclay is dead now. But he was my dad's age. That was surprising enough, but what's really weird? Nia's husband, Evan, is Barclay's illegitimate son."

"Hang on. Nia's husband's father is the same man who..."

"Knocked up my sister, yes. Small world, huh?" I hold Skye close, kiss her because I can't help myself, then settle in to spill the bitter truth. "The minute we left that office building, I pointed out to my dad that we'd been speaking with our own flesh and blood for the first time ever. He told me it didn't matter and that I should forget her."

"That's horrible. Clearly, you didn't."

"No. It took me a while to find the right way to tell Nia that I'm her brother, but I'm glad I did. But my dad refuses to acknowledge her and he won't say why, just insists that I 'get over it.' The only reason I can figure is that he's either ambivalent—which is unlike him—or embarrassed that he has a biracial daughter."

"So Jina was..."

"African-American." I nod. "I've known for years that my father is human and has flaws. I can forgive him a lot. But if he's opting out of Nia's life because of the color of her skin, I can't live with that. I'd rather not be professionally connected with someone who feels that way. But I'm torn because I love our business. I know it inside and out. Walking away would devastate me. I don't know what to do. My head tells me one thing, my heart another."

"I see it's weighing on you." She presses her lips to my forehead. "But can you really make a decision that affects your whole future without knowing why your dad won't speak to Nia?"

She makes a good point. "I don't know if my anger has dwindled enough to talk to him."

"You have to try."

"I know." I kiss her head. "How did you get so smart?"

"I'm not. But I suspect I'm a little more used to leading with my heart than you."

Skye isn't wrong.

"There's that."

"But I look at it this way: if you're unhappy with your dad for writing off family, I'm not sure you can live with yourself for doing the same without truly knowing his reasons."

"Yep. See? Smart. I don't have a good argument against that."

She smiles. "Maybe you shouldn't try to come up with one, either."

I bend to take her mouth again…and my lips start wandering down her neck, then toward the luscious, rosy peaks of her breasts. "I can think of something I'd rather do right now, anyway. Want to see if the sex was really as amazing as we remember?"

"Yes." She arches toward me with a moan. "I do."

* * * *

The following afternoon, I'm hanging out on the lanai, more than half hoping Skye will come back soon. Shortly after breakfast, she disappeared to run errands for her bosses, Dean and Erma, who don't drive much since they're in their eighties.

With her gone, I've been thinking, trying to figure out my life. I venture to peek at the voicemails I've been ignoring, including another one from David Chang. There's also a cheery invitation from Nia, asking me over for dinner tonight to celebrate the birth of Maxon and Keeley Reed's daughter, Kailani, on New Year's Day.

The rest of the messages are from business contacts reaching out to me for other potential deals, which tells me that if I branch off on my own I stand a good chance of being self-sustaining.

The remaining three are from my dad, each more insistent than the last. He's never been good at back-and-forth conversation, just making demands.

In the past, I've always put our business first. Right now, I have to think about a future that suits *me*.

Since it's Monday morning in Hong Kong, I dial Chang. He answers on the first ring.

"Hi, David." His given name is a lot more difficult to pronounce, but for simplicity's sake he's David to his American and British contacts.

"Do you have information for me about the Maui property?" he asks in a slightly British clip, though I still hear a slight Asian enunciation to his tone.

"I do. I've walked the beach, driven the roads, inquired about zoning, building codes, water, sewer…pretty much asked the gamut of questions before one commits to building a hotel." This isn't my first rodeo, after all. "Of course, the property in question isn't actually for sale."

"It's not, but you know the unwritten rule."

"Everything has a price."

"Exactly." I hear the smile in Chang's voice.

"The building codes will present some challenges. Maui has a labyrinth of regulations, most of which aren't conducive to skyscrapers."

"I'm aware of that. I'm challenging my architect to sketch his preliminary designs around that, while making it as profitable as possible. Once that's done, we'll see if the project is worth the return. Tell me about the sellers."

"They're an elderly couple who leave the day-to-day operations of the vacation rental to an employee." It's on the tip of my tongue to point out that we'll displace Skye and eliminate her job if this hotel comes to fruition. But I bite the words back. David won't care. If I didn't know Skye so personally, I wouldn't either.

I feel more than a tad guilty that I'm having this conversation without first speaking to her about this. But she doesn't own the property. Her allegiance is to Dean and Erma, and I can't risk her tipping them off before David is ready to negotiate. Heck, *if* he's ever ready. This whole thing could easily fall apart.

"They have to know they're sitting on a fortune in land," David muses.

Totally. And I'm sure people have made them offers in the past. There must be some reason they haven't sold… Not wanting to lose their home? Or their business? Do they have a sentimental attachment to the place? Something else entirely? Again, none of my business and not my first concern. If David wants to buy the property and he wants help negotiating, I'm there for him.

The conversation today is simply about the feasibility of getting a deal done.

"Probably. We only met for five minutes, so I don't have a sense of them, unfortunately. We'd just have to find their price and see if it's something you can live with."

"But your initial impression is that I should green light this project?"

Completely objectively, without mixing Skye into the equation? "Yes."

"Excellent. I'll tell the others here, and we'll start determining if we want to take the next steps. Will you be calling your father to bring him in?"

I hesitate. "Would it change anything if I didn't?"

"No. You and I have worked together enough that I'm confident I know the service you'll provide. Are you thinking of leaving Colossus?"

I don't dare give David—or anyone—an inch of scoop until I'm ready to make a decision. "No. Just looking to develop some individual elements to my résumé. You never know what the future will bring."

"Those words are both wise and true. I'll be in touch."

"I'll be happy to help in any way I can, David."

He ends the call, and I darken my screen, shoving the device in my pocket and staring out at the placid blue ocean. I'm more than ready for the peace part of my vacation to start. But it won't. I'm bothered by my conversation with David. I'm worried about how our deal could impact Skye. On the other hand, I'm also worried that if I don't pursue this hard it will adversely affect my future, especially if I choose not to go back to New York and resume my position at Colossus.

If I leave the firm, most people will think I'm crazy. Douglas Lund is a financial genius. In my defense, I'm no slouch. Admittedly, I've learned everything from my dad. But everyone knows that one day, probably in the next half-dozen years, he intends to hand me control of his multi-billion dollar business. I've worked all my life to learn his methods and earn his trust. Walking away now may look nonsensical on the surface. But in my gut, it's a viable option. And this deal with David Chang, who is notoriously particular, would totally get me off the ground and bring me some individual Wall Street cred. I might need it since continuing to work with my dad is hitting all my moral buttons.

It's not okay that he won't acknowledge his own fucking daughter. Half of her DNA is his. God, I hope he isn't the sort of man to shut Nia out of his life for the reason I fear. If he is, it's completely unacceptable.

Can you really make a decision that affects your whole future without knowing why your dad won't speak to Nia? Skye asks again in my head.

The slamming of a car door interrupts my reverie. I snap around in my lounger to see Skye loping down the hill at a gait much closer to a run than a walk. Finn's mother is right behind her.

"I don't have anything else to say, Sherry. I'm working right now. But the bottom line is, your son is married. I'm engaged. Finn and I aren't getting back together."

"I don't see your ring," the woman says, her voice carrying on the breeze.

"I took it off when I dipped French toast in batter this morning. Not that it matters. Finn is happy with Dana."

"He's fooled himself. He needs you. That girl is going to bleed his bank account dry."

Skye whirls on Sherry. "Why would you think that? She loves him. She didn't quit her job, and she's never made him buy her things simply because he could."

"She will." The woman sniffs.

"What are you basing this on? Because you think her tattoos make her a gold digger? An immoral whore?"

"Nice girls don't look like that."

"The antiquated notion of a 'nice girl' no longer exists. We're all just women." Skye sounds exhausted by this conversation, probably because it's not the first time they've had it.

"This thing with Dana won't work out, mark my words."

"It's not a thing; it's a *marriage*. They've committed their lives to one another. Until death do they part."

"Ha! I know good attorneys who can fix that. And once the ink is dry on Finn's divorce decree, I'm sure he'll see the light. All I'm asking is that you keep yourself available."

I've heard enough, so I stand and make my way along the lanai, to the side of the house, closing in on the two of them.

"Skye won't be doing that. She's mine." I stop along the side of the house, crossing my arms over my chest, my voice insistent. "Regardless of what happens with your son and his wife, Skye will marry *me*—no one else. I appreciate that you care for her, but she can't fake her feelings for your son for your benefit."

Sherry looks even more agitated. "Maybe she has feelings for you, but she loves Finn."

"As a *friend*," Skye points out, clearly exasperated. "We rarely kissed unless it was for your benefit. We both tried so hard to make it work to please you, but neither of us could fake it. I always knew that he would find someone wonderful for him. If you take away the ink and the bold hair, Dana is a vet tech who loves animals, donates her time to animal-related causes, and helps run a mobile vet service to help make sure all the island's pets have good medical care. Why wouldn't you love a woman with such a big heart?"

"Because she's not you."

I step off the lanai and do my best impression of a casual walk toward them, until I put myself between Skye and Sherry. "I appreciate that you see just how wonderful Skye is, but she has to follow her heart, just like your son does. They've both decided their hearts belong with different significant others."

Sherry's eyes narrow. "You appeared so suddenly in Skye's life. She never mentioned a word about you before this week. So how permanent can you really be? And why are you staying in the Aloha Rainbow rental, instead of with your girlfriend at her place?"

"Fiancée," I correct automatically.

"Whatever. Why wouldn't you stay with her?"

"My place is too cramped," Skye insists, her voice strong. I'm proud of her for the improvisational excuse. "Stephen isn't a small man, and my barely more-than-twin bed isn't big enough for us both."

"Besides, I'm here on vacation. Dean and Erma had a last-minute opening, which allows me to be closer and more romantic with Skye." I lean in. "I understand you're unhappy with your son's choice of bride, but you can't make my fiancée miserable because of it. I think it would be better for us all if you let Skye and I enjoy our evening."

Sherry sniffs. "You're asking me to leave?"

I try to give her a good-natured smile. "After Finn and Dana's lovely wedding, we realize we have a lot of planning to do on our own before I head back to New York."

Finn's mother leans around me to look at Skye. "Are you really okay with him throwing me off the property?"

"That's not how you should look at it. We're just—"

"On our way to meet my sister and her husband for dinner." I step back and put my arm around Skye with a smile. "Nia is looking forward to meeting you, too. So we should get going."

"Yeah." Skye's smile is more stilted than I'd like, but she does her best to warm to the topic. "Just let me put the groceries away."

"I'll text Nia that we'll be there in an hour, then give you a hand." Then I turn to Finn's mother. "Good to see you, Sherry. Skye and I wish Finn and Dana all the best. I think if you put your energy into doing the same, you'll be much happier."

Sherry doesn't say another word, simply whirls around and storms back to her car, looking far from happy—or ready to give up.

"C'mon." I tug on Skye's hand once we hear Sherry's car back out of its spot and bump its way down the dirt road. "I'll help you with the groceries."

"Thanks. What do you want for dinner? I've got tons of options now, so whatever tempts your taste buds…"

Skye herself tempts my taste buds. I'd love to lay her out across my bed and feast on her all night, but I can tell by the way she's walking that she's still a little tender in all my favorite spots.

It probably makes me a caveman, but I smile.

"I was serious. Nia invited us to dinner."

"Us? Does she even know about me?"

Not yet, but she will. "Sure. Game for meeting her?"

Skye nibbles on that lip I love to kiss so much. "Y-you want me to meet her?"

I know what she's asking, if my feelings are actually so strong that I want to introduce her to family.

"Yeah." I tuck a strand of hair behind her ear and kiss her. "I'd love that."

She smiles. "I'd like that, too."

Within a few minutes, we've situated everything she bought at the store. Afterward, Skye changes into a sundress, fluffs her hair, tosses on some mascara and lip gloss, then settles herself in the front seat of my rental car. I'm still chuckling, thinking about Nia's response to my text that I was bringing a date.

There's some matchmaking in my future. And I'm actually happy about it. When it comes to swaying Skye in my favor, I'm all about an unfair advantage.

Ten minutes later, we pull up in front of a lovely white house sprawling in the bright, tropical sun. Nia greets us at the door, wearing a vibrant coral sundress and a smile. Evan is right behind her in shorts and a Hawaiian shirt, hand resting possessively on her hip.

"Hey! Glad you made it." She hugs me.

I'm thrilled to see that she looks happier than ever. It was touch and go between her and Evan for a while. He'd been a widower, and the fact Nia was his assistant complicated their relationship. Throw some jealousy and an unexpected pregnancy into the mix...

"Thanks for inviting us. Nia, Evan, this is Skye Ingram."

My sister and her husband give my girl a warm welcome, and we all head inside, past the fireplace that's thoroughly impractical in Maui, but Evan got it for Nia anyway because she wanted it so badly. The look on my sister's face tells me she now has everything she's ever dreamed of.

As they lead us through the gorgeous house and toward the lanai out back, Nia grabs Skye's arm. "Is my brother behaving himself?"

She glances over her shoulder at me, clearly not sure how to answer. I see the flush crawling up her cheeks. I have no doubt Evan and Nia will, too.

My sister laughs. "I'll take that as a no. But you're here with him, so I'm guessing that means you still like him despite his bad behavior."

"Yeah." Skye smiles. "Actually, he's been really wonderful."

Her voice sounds soft. I hear the happiness in it, and it does something to me. My cock, of course. It's always attuned to her. But this feeling resides farther north, in my chest. I love the idea of being the man who makes Skye truly happy.

No idea why or how that would actually work, but there it is. And the suspicion that I've fallen for her deepens.

"We've had a good time. She's fantastic," I tell Nia.

That makes Skye blush more, but she soldiers on. "I hear you're new to the island? I've lived here my whole life, so if you need any recommendations on things to do or places to eat..."

"That would be great. All of us would love a good pedicurist."

"All of us?" Skye blinks.

We step outside, under the shade of the overhang, to find a long patio table set up with a colorful tablecloth, a hodgepodge of chairs...and every member of Evan's extended family waiting for us.

"Good to see you!" Maxon stands and shoves his hand in my direction.

As we shake, I see his pretty redhead of a wife cradling their newborn daughter. Beyond her sleepy expression, she glows with happiness.

"You, too. Congratulations. Your daughter is beautiful."

"Isn't she?" Keeley, Maxon's wife, says. "Too bad she's got her daddy's disposition."

Maxon laughs. "She does. Impatient all the time. She wants everything now and she wants it perfect."

"That's it." Keeley nods. "God help me."

Skye smiles beside me. "She's beautiful. How old is she?"

"Two weeks today. You must be Skye." When my girl nods, Keeley fills her in. "Nia told us about you. Would you like to hold her?"

"I'd love to."

"Let me introduce her to everyone real quick," Nia puts in, then points to the blonde beside Keeley. "That's Britta, Griff's wife. They're parents to that rug rat out there." She points to a toddler running with abandon through the sprinklers on the far side of the yard.

"And this one." Britta lays a hand on her very pregnant belly. "Who needs to come out already."

"Congratulations. When are you due?" Skye asks.

"Two days ago. I'm so miserable."

Griff kisses her head and laughs as he sticks his hand in Skye's direction. "That's how I know our second son will be like his mommy. She's always late."

Britta sticks a good-natured tongue out at him.

He winks back at his wife. "But if you want to try kickstarting your labor again, I'll be happy to take you home and put that tongue to good use."

The prim little blonde turns twenty shades of red and slaps at her husband with a little tsk. Everyone around them laughs.

"It's nice to meet you both." Skye shakes their hands, then looks between the brothers. "I've seen your billboards all over the island for the last few months. This is kind of like meeting celebrities."

Nia laughs. "Reed Brothers Property Associates is doing really well—"

"Number one in Maui," Maxon puts in.

"We're a killer team," Griff finishes with pride.

"Mostly because you're both stubborn and don't take no for an answer," Britta chimes in.

Everyone laughs.

"But if you want a celebrity, meet this guy." My sister points across the table at a hulk of an athlete. "Noah Weston, legendary NFL quarterback and hall-of-famer."

"Retired and it will be five years before I'm even eligible for a vote."

My sister scoffs. "You're a shoo-in."

"Thank you." Noah turns his attention to me. "Good to see you, man."

"You, too."

"And you're Skye? Pretty name."

"Thank you. It's nice to meet you." She winces. "Sorry. I know nothing about football."

Noah just smiles. "Neither did my wife when we first met. She was totally unimpressed. So I had to marry her. This is Harlow." He bumps shoulders with his wife. "Since we're having a baby in three weeks, I think I appropriately dazzled her."

"Maybe, big guy. Maybe…" The gorgeous brunette wearing the enormous rock extends her hand to Skye with a laugh. "Great to meet you."

"Same. Congratulations. Is this baby your first?"

She nods. "I'm so ready."

"I'll say. If you decorate the nursery with any more shit, the weight of it all will send the second floor collapsing into the first."

Harlow elbows him. "Ha! Even you admitted it's cute in there."

"It's adorable," Keeley says. "I wish I had half your talent for decorating."

"You do," Harlow insists. "I love Kailani's nursery."

"I haven't even started my nursery," Nia puts in with a groan. "Thank goodness I have time."

"One-hundred-ninety-six days," Evan confirms, already looking nervous.

"It sounds so far away." My sister rubs her still flat belly affectionately. "I just want to cuddle our little munchkin now."

"Everyone here is expecting? Remind me not to drink the water." Skye laughs.

"Hey, we're all newlyweds." Maxon shrugs. "Besides, I have to catch up to Griff in the daddy department."

Keeley turns to him, brow raised. "My uterus is not here for you to win some juvenile game with your brother."

"Of course not, sunshine. I love you so much. And I'll do my very best to sweet-talk you into another baby as soon as the doctor says it's okay…"

"Oh, I know you'll try." She sighs. "Fatherhood has not made you any less relentless."

Everyone laughs again.

It's a close-knit group. I know in the last year they've all overcome tremendous difficulties and fought unbelievable pain to find happiness.

At the end of the table, I see the two stragglers who haven't managed that feat yet.

"Hey, I didn't know you'd be here, Trace." I wave at him.

"Yeah. Ranger and I hopped in the car when we heard you were coming." He cradles a newborn in a blue onesie with one arm and holds a bottle to the baby's little working mouth with the other. "Good to see you. I'd shake your hand, but someone is a demanding eater."

I laugh, then turn to Skye. "This is Noah's brother, Trace. And his son, Ranger."

Trace nods in greeting. "We're the bachelors of the group, along with this guy next to me. What was your name again?"

It's obvious Trace is teasing, and the man in question rolls his eyes. "Bite my ass."

Trace tsks. "Your parents should really have rethought that moniker. Then again, it fits."

The gathering erupts in laughter once more.

The tall man stands, smile tight, looking a little out of place. "Sebastian Shaw. I'm Evan's CFO and bestie."

"Good to meet you." I shake his hand.

Skye does the same. "Are you visiting the island?"

He shakes his head. "I moved here, just a few miles up the road, when Evan relocated his company a few weeks ago. I'm still getting acclimated."

"It's a big change from Seattle for all of us," Nia puts in. "So far, Bas isn't a fan of the singles' scene around here."

"What singles' scene?" he quips.

"Have a seat." Nia points to two empty chairs at the table sandwiched between Bas and her own.

As Skye and I settle in, my sister plays hostess, getting us drinks, answering the doorbell when the caterer arrives, and making sure everyone is happy and comfortable. There's lots of food, teasing, and laughter all around the table.

When the meal is over, the men gravitate toward the pool near the back end of the yard, talking about the NFL playoffs and the remaining teams' strengths and weaknesses, along with the fact Noah would be providing color commentary this week if it weren't for the fact that Harlow—along with Maxon, Griff, Evan, and my friend Bethany—lost their father a few days ago. His funeral is in San Diego on Tuesday.

The fact that no one is in mourning says more about Barclay Reed than them.

"Have you talked to Bethany?" Maxon asks me quietly as the other men chatter on.

I nod. "On Friday. She's doing all right. Just busy."

"She has a lot on her plate."

I nod again. "She sends her love."

"Back at her. Any change between her and Clint?"

I shake my head. "She needs time."

"And she needs to get Dad in the ground before she can move on. I get it. I hope she and Clint make it. They're perfect for each other."

I agree. "Yeah. Barclay was your father, too. How are you holding up? And the rest of your siblings?"

Maxon scoffs. "My dad burned bridges with me long ago, so as far as I was concerned he was already dead. I'm mostly going to the son of a bitch's funeral to support Bethany." He grimaces. "You've known her a lot longer than I have, but she's still our sister. She's worshipped Dad for a long time, so she's still hurting."

"Yeah." Barclay and all his fucked-up affairs have created a really complicated family tree. And I hate to even bring this up… "I don't know if you know, but my sister, Amanda, has a son, Oliver."

"I'm glad you brought it up. He's our brother, too. As far as we're concerned, he'll always be welcome with the Reed clan. If your sister is amenable, we'd like to meet Oliver and be a part of his life."

"I think Amanda would like that. She's lost and afraid right now. She doesn't love Barclay anymore." That misplaced case of hero worship had damn near ruined her life. "But I think it hit her hard when she realized her child will never really know his father."

"Then we're happy to represent the Reeds."

"I appreciate that, especially since you all are the best parts of that bastard."

"Thanks." Maxon looks over his shoulder toward his wife and

daughter, but I see him taking Skye in as she laughs and chats like she belongs. "So…what's the deal with you two?"

It's so complicated, I don't even know where to start. I give him the minimum. "We met on Tuesday. She needed a date to her ex-boyfriend's wedding yesterday, so I took her."

He gives me a sly smile. "Not merely out of the goodness of your heart. You're into her. It's all over your face."

I watch Skye sip some cocktail the ladies have tossed together and begged her to try for them because she's the only woman not pregnant. Her eyes widen in delight, and I smile. My feelings probably are obvious. I'm usually good at keeping them in. I'm great at poker and even better at business. But Skye turns me inside out.

When I turn back to answer Maxon, I see all the men waiting on my every word. "Do you blame me?"

Every man there shakes his head.

"She seems really sweet," Griff remarks as Keeley hands Skye a sleeping Kailani.

My girl's face lights up.

What would it be like to see her holding our baby?

I'll probably never know. One of the things Skye picked up while she was out this morning was condoms, and being safe would be smarter for us both…but I'll miss taking her bare. And even though it makes no sense, I regret not having the opportunity to tie myself to her in a lasting way.

You could just propose.

After four days? When I have no idea where my life is going?

"Harlow already likes her," Noah puts in. "I can tell. And she's an excellent judge of character."

Griff scoffed. "No, she's not. She married you."

"Fuck off." Noah tosses him a mock punch.

"You first." Griff blocks with his elbow, then runs after his drenched son, still playing in the wet grass, even though the sprinklers have cut off.

Noah follows, and they both chase a happily screaming Jamie.

"If Skye makes you happy, that would make Nia happy," Evan puts in.

I already know that for straightforward Evan, little else matters to him. It's one reason my half-sister loves him so much.

"So far, she does. Thanks."

"Evan!" Nia calls from the bar. "Can you go get a couple more bags of ice out of the freezer? We're empty out here."

"On it." He turns to Maxon and me. "Excuse me."

The second he's gone, the eldest of the Reed siblings turns to me. "So…a birdie tells me you're scouting a property on the island for potential hotel development."

That sends my gaze whizzing back around. "How did you hear?"

"You're kidding, right? Griff and I basically own real estate transactions on this island."

"Residential."

"We're starting to dabble in commercial. That land? It isn't for sale."

I raise a brow. "When has that ever stopped anyone?"

Maxon gives me a tight smile. "Let me put it this way: I have a client in Honolulu who tried to buy it about two years ago for roughly the same purposes. The Abelsons refused to even entertain an offer."

That isn't good news. David Chang won't be happy. "Why?"

"I'm putting two and two together now… Does your Skye work for them? Has she for a while?"

"Yeah." I frown. "How did you know that?"

Maxon grimaces like he hates to be the bearer of bad news. "The Abelsons said they'd never sell because they're leaving the land and the house to their caretaker, the girl who's been like a daughter to them. If memory serves, they said her name was Skye."

CHAPTER FOUR

Saturday, February 3

Nearly three weeks slide by, and now I'm beginning to sweat. Being with Skye is so, so easy. In fact, it's the best part of being on Maui, which is absolutely perfect…except the part where I feel like I'm lying to her. But what can I do? David Chang hasn't said he either wants to move forward or halt the hotel project. And I don't have any idea whether Maxon's bombshell is accurate or just an excuse the Abelsons gave to the last unwanted buyer. I can't ask them; they flew to San Francisco to be with Erma's older brother—almost ninety—who's having surgery. They won't be back for weeks. And I don't know whether Skye has any idea if the elderly couple intends to leave their property to her. Asking her opens a can of worms I should keep closed. And admitting this pending development both betrays Chang's confidence and potentially blows up our relationship for a deal that may fall apart tomorrow.

It's a tangle.

"What are you going to do?" Maxon asks on the other end of the phone.

"Fuck if I know."

I've been trying like hell to find other suitable commercially zoned properties on the island for sale. I've sent David all kinds of listings, everything from budget-busting eye-catching ocean vistas to smaller acreage with mountain views and really motivated sellers. He's turned down each one. He wants *this* land. And I know why. It will literally be the most amazing—and lucrative—slice of paradise.

I'm getting desperate.

"I can keep looking," Maxon offers.

"No. It's okay, man," I tell him. "You're short-handed with Britta still out on maternity leave and Griff only working half days. Besides, the client isn't going to budge. If he proceeds, he won't settle for any property but this one."

"Then you've got some decisions to make."

No shit. I'm only here another week and I still haven't decided if I want to resume my old life in New York or start over on my own somewhere else, like Maui. If I leave Colossus to stay here, I'll need this deal to become a major player.

"Yeah."

"You want to talk about it?" Maxon lets loose an annoyed huff. "Jesus, I sound like my wife. What the fuck is happening? I'm volunteering to talk about emotions…"

I laugh. "You don't have to. I'd hate to be the reason you break out in hives."

"These days, it's just a mild itch. I couldn't be married to Keeley if I was unable to handle the touchy-feely shit. Here's the thing… I think you love this girl."

"It's that obvious?"

I'm in love. And I keep falling. Every day, every night. I'm happier with Skye than I've ever been. We've developed our own routine, which I adore. We sleep in—something I haven't done since college. After breakfast, we walk along the beach. I spend mid-morning working, tidying the loose ends I didn't mop up before leaving New York and cultivating potential new deals while Skye takes care of the property, including the Abelsons' place, then runs errands. I fix myself lunch. She appears again about three. Sometimes we have a snack. Sometimes I just have her. Wine, dinner, talk, followed by another mind-blowing night in bed that I swear just keeps getting hotter and better.

By unspoken agreement, neither of us brings up the future. We don't know what it will bring. But I do know that after I mailed the faux engagement ring back to my friend's friend, I missed seeing it on Skye's finger. That's probably my first clue… Second, I keep looking at my plane ticket back to New York and dreading next Saturday.

On the other hand, I've spoken to my father a couple of times. He says he wants to discuss business, that it's important. I tell him I want to talk about Nia first. He insists that subject isn't up for discussion. We end our calls at a chilly impasse. It's unfinished shit, and I can't leave it dangling like a turd from the butt crack of our relationship. This has to get wiped and flushed before I can truly decide where my future lies.

I hear a knock at the front door and glance at my phone. It's just after two in the afternoon, early for Skye, but maybe she's got groceries and needs a hand.

"Coming!" I leap from the lounger on the lanai and set my laptop aside, lumbering through the house in a tank top, shorts, and bare feet before I open the door.

The last person I expect to see standing there is my dad.

"Hi, Stephen."

"Hi. What are you doing here? I didn't expect you."

He nods. "I wanted to surprise you. Can I come in?"

"Yeah." I step back, still in shock. I haven't seen him for nearly a month. As much as I don't respect his attitude toward Nia, I love my dad and I've missed him like hell. "Of course. I was just out on the lanai."

I turn and lead the way. He follows me through the house, then outside, his stare glued to the gentle roll of the blue, blue ocean. "This is beautiful. No wonder you're liking it here. And you've got a tan in February." He gives me a wry little laugh. "It looks good on you."

Dad looks New-York-winter white. And so damn tired.

"Thanks. Did you fly all night to get here?"

"Pretty much."

Then whatever he has to say is serious. "Can I get you something to drink? Eat?"

Vaguely, I realize I'm stalling. Dad never does anything without careful planning and forethought. There's always a reason for everything, and I'm almost afraid to hear his. He can be a ruthless SOB when it comes to business. Has he come here to issue me some ultimatum, like come home now or walk away with nothing?

"No, thank you." He sits in the chair across from my lounger.

I close the lid to my laptop, filled with notes about the very property we're on, sit down, and give him my full attention. "Actually, I'm glad you came."

He sighs tiredly. "You want to talk about Nia."

I nod. "And I presume you want to talk about business."

"Yes." He steeples his fingers like he's getting ready to launch into some argument he means to persuade me to his way of thinking.

I cut him off. "Here's the thing, Dad: I can only think of one reason why you won't talk to Nia, and I hate to think your soul is that ugly."

He frowns, then understanding dawns. "You think I'm a racist. Jesus... I really have fucked this up."

"Give me one good reason to think something else." I'm basically pleading. "Anything else."

"This is the way Jina wanted things."

Of all the things my dad could have said, I didn't expect that. "Come again?"

He blows out a harsh breath. "Nothing more awkward than vomiting up your personal life to your son... Look, it's no secret your mom and I had been miserable for a long time, but she wasn't about to give up the money, the country club, and all her pretentious friends."

"No surprise." My mom loved me...in her way. But she seemed equally passionate about her fancy friends and fancy life. "But what does that have to do with Nia's mother?"

"Jina worked for us, lived in our house. You were young; maybe you don't remember."

"I do." Vaguely.

Dad hesitates. "We became...friends."

"Obviously more than friends since you two conceived Nia."

"But we were friends first. For years. She knew I didn't love your mother. She also knew your mother would string me up by the balls financially if I divorced her." He hesitates again, the pause almost uncomfortably long. "I knew she was in love with me. Eventually, I fell for her, too. I would have given anything to marry her. But after your mother got pregnant with Amanda—"

"It takes two to tango," I point out.

"It does. And I take responsibility. In retrospect, I think your mother knew I was falling for Jina and tried to convince me that what we needed to really be a happy family was another baby. It was stupid, and I felt so guilty for wanting Jina. At that point, I'd never touched her...but I wanted to and she knew it. So did your mother."

"So you capitulated and tried to be the good husband?"

He nods. "I tried so hard. But after her first trimester, she told me this baby was her insurance policy to remaining my wife. If the divorce settlement didn't kill me financially, the child support would. Then she kicked me out of bed." He grimaces. "I was furious that she manipulated my guilt and I let her play me…but in a way I was relieved, too. I knew where my heart was."

"Jina."

"Yes. We had a great couple of months. I was up front and told her I couldn't divorce your mother. At first she accepted that, but as time went on it became a strain between us. When she realized she was pregnant, we both knew things couldn't continue as they had been. Your mother found out about the baby and made our lives hell. We both agreed it would be best for the child if she left and raised our daughter elsewhere." He closes his eyes and presses a hand to his forehead. "Letting them go broke my fucking heart."

"So Jina moved to Georgia, then. Did you ever see her again?"

"The day Nia was born. I flew out there and held Jina's hand while she went through labor. I'd hoped the fact that she asked me to come meant… But it didn't. I got to spend an hour holding Nia." His eyes water as he grinds his jaw shut, trying to hold back the tears. "That's it. Then Jina asked me to leave. A month later, she sent me legal paperwork, insisting I sign away my parental rights. The pregnancy was so unexpected, and I couldn't walk away from my other responsibilities. I couldn't give her anything but money and peace, so I gave her what she asked for. One of her terms was that I had to agree never to contact Nia in the future. And she was never to know my name."

"Why?"

"Honestly, Jina was bitter. She was convinced I would have married her if she had been white or from the right family or something other than a maid. I laughed when she told me that. She didn't think it was funny." He rakes a hand through his hair. "I was fucking trapped. Your mother made sure that the only way I could divorce her was if I gave up everything, including the legacy I intended to leave you. I paid a steep price to keep everything together. But if I had to do it over again, knowing what I know now… I would have chosen Jina. I spent the rest of my fucking life miserable without her. It was even worse, knowing she learned to hate me. Just like I'm sure her daughter does."

Jesus, that's sad. I swallow a lump in my throat. But my dad isn't without fault. Yes, my mother and Nia's made his life miserable, but he chose money and ambition over his heart. "Nia doesn't hate you. She thinks you're convinced she's not good enough. She thinks you don't want her because she's biracial."

My dad closes his eyes and shakes his head. "Everyone assumes they know why I've kept my distance—and it's the worst reason imaginable—but they're so fucking far off the mark. I don't actually know that woman as a person, but I know so much about my daughter on paper. I'm proud of what she's accomplished. She's smart. She's beautiful. She's funny, I hear. She's got gumption. In so many ways, she reminds me of Jina…"

My dad looks so close to losing it that I can't not approach him. We've never been an affectionate family, but I feel like he needs a hug. Or maybe I've just gotten used to how often Skye has her arms around me now and it feels natural to comfort someone so mired in anguish.

"I'm sorry, Dad. I should never have thought the worst." It hurt him; I can tell.

I'm shocked when he stands and hugs me back in a tight, back-slapping embrace, then eases away with a ragged sigh. "And I shouldn't have been such a proud, stubborn ass. I should have reached out to Nia after Jina died. If she had rejected me…well, I would have known, right? Instead, the wondering has tormented me for three fucking years."

"Do you want to see her? Is that why you flew all the way to Maui?"

"I came to talk to you…but I would like to see her. She and Cook are expecting a baby, I hear."

"At the end of July." I try to lighten the mood. "Feel like being a grandpa again?"

He nods, a laugh bubbling up. "God, I sound old. Then again, I feel old."

Dad is in his late fifties, but he's in great shape and he's got a lot of life left. But if what he's said is true, he's been playing a really shitty hand for a couple of decades. Maybe we can fix that. I think Nia would at least hear him out.

"How are Amanda and Oliver?"

"Good. She took the news of Barclay's death better than I expected." He eyes me. "If you decide to stay, she'll probably come visit you."

I'd like that. I think she'd fit right in with the Reed clan and all their babies. *If* I decide to stay.

"Honestly, I'm not sure what I'm doing next yet." Now that I know my dad's refusal to see Nia has nothing to do with the color of her skin, my decision should be easy, right? I should be jumping at the chance to return to New York and resume my high-powered career.

I'm not.

"I know why you're here and what you're contemplating. Let me make this easier for you, son." He sighs. "Barclay's death reminded me that life is short. Despite everything he stole from me, I still have a lot of money, and I'm tired of the game. What I'm not tired of? Family. I've spent so little with any of my kids, especially my daughters. I want to make things right with all of you."

My heart starts pounding. Is he saying what I think he's saying? "Are you...retiring?"

I have a hard time asking the question. My dad has talked about it off and on over the years like something in the distant future, but the truth is I never actually pictured him following through.

"I'd like to. I'll stay around in an advisory position until the IPO is over so we don't rock the boat and affect the price of the initial stock offering, but essentially I want you to take over, effective February twelfth."

In nine days? *Holy shit.*

"You look shocked," Dad drawls.

"Um...huge understatement."

"I'm sure. But since you left, I've been thinking. This makes the most sense for us all. If you'll think about it, you know that's true." My dad claps me on the shoulder. "What do you say, son?"

It's everything I've worked for all my life. My father is giving it to me on a silver fucking platter years before I thought he'd concede that I'd earned it. I'll be a major Wall Street player before I'm thirty-five. I'll be a billionaire before I'm forty. I'll be able to write my own ticket for the rest of my life. It's a dream come true.

But Skye, my Hawaiian girl, will never come to New York with me no matter how much money I'm worth. Accepting my dad's offer will mean leaving her behind. It will mean ripping my heart in two.

I don't know what the fuck to do.

"I need a drink." I head inside and head straight for the decorative booze cart in the living room. Scotch isn't going to solve anything, but it will help me process this oh-fuck-me shock.

Head or heart? That's essentially the choice in front of me.

Whatever I do will have enormous ramifications on my future.

But hey, no pressure. We're just talking the rest of your life...

Suddenly, I hear the front door open, then shut carefully. Skye. How am I going to introduce her to my father?

I don't hear footsteps or a greeting or any noise. She's absolutely silent. The hairs on the back of my neck prickle. She's a lot of things, but quiet isn't one of them.

Setting my drink on the cart, I run to intercept her in the entryway. I'm desperate to touch her, hold her, have one more minute before everything changes. Goddamn it, I'm not ready for Skye to meet my father. No, that's not it. I'm not ready for him to meet her, for him to know precisely why I'm not celebrating his potential retirement or immediately accepting his offer to become CEO. This secret is mine. *She's* mine. I don't want him trying to talk me out of her—and he will. I want to keep Skye to myself until I can figure this conundrum out.

But when I round the corner, she stands rooted in place with her purse hanging limply from her shoulder, an expression that says her world has fallen apart, and tears streaming down her surprisingly pale face.

"Honey?" In that moment, I forget everything except her. I scoop her in my arms to console her.

She shakes her head and backs away. "I-I'm sorry. I'm so…"

When her sentence dissolves into tears, I'm really confused. What has she done but love me and show me what meaningful relationships should be? "Honey, you have nothing to be sorry for."

Is she worried that I don't love her? I haven't told her yet. I haven't admitted that I've been seriously thinking of proposing for real. I haven't confessed that I don't want to live without her by my side.

What the hell am I going to choose?

She nods miserably. "Yes, I do. I told you it would be okay and…" She covers her face with her hands.

Even though I'm frantically trying to figure out what the fucking problem is, I can't not hold her. "Whatever it is I'm sure we can fix it, honey. It will be fine."

"It won't. And you can't just fix it," she hurls with another sob. "I'm pregnant."

* * * *

My father steps into the house from the lanai and looks at me across the empty feet between us, shock freezing his expression. *Shit.* He overheard everything.

And he's already wondering where my loyalties—and my future—lie.

When she sees my dad, her eyes flare wide. Horror fills her face. I haven't introduced them, but my father and I look enough alike that she can certainly guess who he is.

"Oh." She tries to back away. "I'm so sorry. I didn't…"

I curl my arm around her back to stay her. "Skye, this is my dad, Douglas."

She swipes at the mascara running down her face and lifts her chin bravely. "It's nice to meet you."

I'm proud of the way she tries to brazen it out.

My dad holds out his hand, and I'm glad when she takes it. "Likewise, Skye. Stephen, I'll leave you two to talk. Call me."

Because he needs an answer soon. As if Skye's pronouncement didn't throw a major monkey wrench into my whole life.

"Yeah." I can't say anything else right now.

I'm relieved when the door shuts behind my dad, leaving me alone with my girl. And our baby.

Holy shit.

"I'm so sorry. I-I didn't know he was…"

Here? Obviously. "I didn't know he was coming, either." And that's not what's important right now. "Are you sure about the baby, honey?"

Skye simply nods. "I noticed my breasts have been weirdly achy for the past couple of days. Then I realized my period should have started almost a week ago. I took a home test."

I don't argue the accuracy of the test just now, mostly because I remember when Amanda realized she was pregnant. Same symptoms. If Skye were any other woman, I'd wonder if she was making this up for the money. But that's not who she is. I knew going in bare was a risk. At the time, I didn't care.

If you had a do-over on that day would you choose anything different?

Right now, I don't know.

"Let's get you seen by a doctor." Just in case she's the one percent that's inaccurate.

She swipes at her tears again. "That will take days."

Usually, yeah. But I'm counting on Nia and her family by marriage. With that many pregnant women, surely someone's doctor can fit her in.

"Give me a minute." But I can't walk away when Skye looks like she's falling apart, so I lead her to a chair, sit her down, and kiss her forehead. "Breathe, honey."

"You aren't shocked?"

"I am. But we'll figure it out."

Then I walk out of the room, debating who to call. Nia is the obvious choice, but she'll ask questions, want details, and probably put in her two cents. I need someone who will be emotionless and cut to the chase.

After scrolling through my contacts, I hit a button to dial the perfect person. He answers on the first ring. "Hey, Evan. What are you up to?"

"Work."

He's not a great conversationalist. Never has been. I don't take it personally. There's a reason he'd rather talk to computers. "Then I won't keep you. Do you know the name of Nia's obstetrician?"

Dutifully, he recites the woman's name and phone number. "She's usually booked up, but if you need her to see Skye quickly, her nurse practitioner runs a drop-in clinic just down the street."

No one can ever accuse Evan of being slow. Without asking a single question, he seems to have grasped what I need.

"Thanks."

"I assume you don't want me to say anything to your sister?"

"For now, anyway."

"Then as far as I'm concerned, you never called. Goodbye." He hangs up.

I pocket my phone, then return to Skye. She's staring at the wall vacantly. Her news surprised me, but it's clearly freaked her out a hundred times more. I'm not the one who has to endure morning sickness, exhaustion, and all the other hormonal crap that comes with pregnancy. I'm not the one with a physical job that may be somewhere between difficult and impossible to do once she's in her third trimester. I'm not the one who has to go through childbirth.

Are you going to help her raise this child? Or choose your career?

I grimace. Those are questions I can't answer yet. One step at a time.

My dad wants me to think about his offer. Right now, all I can think about is Skye.

With slow steps, I gather my shit and approach, crouching in front of her and taking her hands. "I think I can get you seen by someone this afternoon. Once we've gotten some answers, we'll talk."

She hesitates, then nods. "Let me clean up."

Skye disappears into the bathroom for a few minutes. I hear running water. Over that, I hears sobs. She's scared.

Fuck, I'm rattled, too. I admit it.

When she finally emerges, she looks red-eyed but surprisingly composed. Hell, almost placid. I'm not fooled, but everything about her body language tells me she doesn't want to talk right now. She's fragile. If I disturb her facade, she might fall apart.

I swallow back my need to hold her and help her into the car instead.

The trip to the clinic is quick, the wait even shorter. A nurse practitioner with a calming demeanor and a kind smile takes Skye to the back and gives her some instructions while leaving me in the waiting room. Less than five minutes later, an assistant opens the door and invites me in.

Skye is there alone, quietly trying to hold herself together. I can't not touch her, so I take her in my arms.

"Honey, it will be all right." It's an empty assurance. I don't know how it will be yet, I just know it has to be.

"You think so? I don't know for sure, but I'm guessing your dad came to Maui to take you back to New York." Her expression dares me to refute her.

I can't. "It's complicated."

Before Skye can say anything, the nurse practitioner, Lydia, enters with the same calm smile and urges us both to sit.

My heart is thudding wildly as I do. I'm on the edge of my seat. I don't even know what I'm hoping for. Life will be less tricky if Skye isn't pregnant.

But will that truly make life better?

My head is a fucked-up jumble. It's as if life woke up this morning and thought it would be a great joke to shake everything up like a bottle of soda, then rip off the cap. No one is laughing, especially not Skye.

I take her hand and squeeze it.

"I have your test results," Lydia says, managing to keep her expression completely neutral. She'd make a hell of a poker player.

"And?" I prompt her along.

She gives me a patient smile, then turns to Skye, reaching out with a gentle hand. "You're pregnant."

The air leaves my lungs. I sit dizzy and stunned in my chair.

Holy. Shit. I'm going to be a father.

All the color leaves Skye's face. "Oh, my god…"

"I see it's a shock. Believe me, you're not the first one to be surprised. Give it a few days to sink in and you'll be fine. Your due date is approximately October sixth. You'll want to follow up with your ob-gyn in the next month. If you time the visit right, you might be far enough along to hear the baby's heartbeat."

Her words slam into me. A heartbeat already?

"O-okay." Skye nods, clearly on auto-pilot.

"Do you have any other questions?" Lydia asks.

Probably a million…and I can't think of a single one right now.

Skye simply shakes her head.

I pay for the office visit as she wanders out the door looking shell-shocked and frozen. I'm only two minutes behind her, but seeing her leaning against my rental car looking so lost pains me.

I can't offer to go back to that night and undo what we did; I can only go forward and take her in my arms.

"Honey, we're going to figure something out."

She blinks up at me, her big brown eyes so full of anguish. "I don't know what that means."

"I don't, either. But we made a human being together. We'll work this out together, too."

She nods absently. "Sorry to be so weepy."

"You're stunned. And hormonal. I've been through this recently with my sister. I get it."

Skye gives me a vacant half smile as I help her into the car.

The ride back is silent. I take her hand. She clutches me in return. It's the only outward sign that she wants anything from me at all.

When we pull up in front of the Aloha Rainbow house, I see an unfamiliar car. Who the fuck is here now?

Beside me, Skye groans. "Sherry? Again?"

I've had enough of this woman. And now is a really shitty time for her tantrum. I'm going to make sure she understands that no means no once and for all.

"Stay here. I'll take care of this."

"No. Finn is my ex, so this is my problem." She's out the passenger door before I can stop her.

I follow.

"There you are," Sherry calls out to Skye over the breeze blowing through the front yard.

"Look, it's been a really long day, and there's a lot going on. I don't want to argue—"

"I'm not surprised." She glares at me. "Did you finally realize your fiancé is using you? I already know. You can come home with me, Skye. I'm sure Finn will rush over to console you."

What. The. Fuck? "She's not going anywhere with you, Sherry. And I'm not using her."

Is this woman delusional?

Skye sighs tiredly. "He's not, but I just found out I'm pregnant, so it would be great if you gave us a little space to—"

"By him?" She points in my direction.

"Yes. Sherry, I never had sex with your son. Not once. We're *friends.*"

She sniffs. "You would have been better off with Finn. This one is only here to sell you out."

"What are you talking about?" I approach, scowling.

"I did some digging about you, mister. I know you come from big New York money. I know you're hailed as some financial genius. I know you help broker deals around the world. But I have friends all over the island who tell me you've been inquiring about the very land we're standing on."

Son of a bitch. "Listen—"

"No, you shut up." Sherry turns to Skye. "He's inquired about changing the zoning on this property, about road and sewage expansion, and about the net value of the land. My guess is he has a client who wants to build a hotel, and he knew the Abelsons would never sell to him, so he cozied up to the only person in the world who could convince them to market the land to someone else. You."

Shock—and yes, betrayal—crosses Skye's face.

I grab Skye's hands in mine. "That's not what happened. Yes, I have a client who asked me to look at the viability of making this land into a hotel. But I'm only asking due diligence questions and—"

"Was having sex with me part of your due diligence, too?"

She's believing Sherry over me?

She's known the woman since she was five. She's known you for less than a month. Who did you think was going to win the credibility battle?

"I had sex with you because I wanted you and you wanted me. I'm still here with you and contemplating giving up my whole future for you and our baby, despite the fact my dad came here today to offer me all I've ever wanted professionally. Every. Single. Thing. And even before I knew about the baby, I didn't jump to say yes to his proposition because I love you."

Skye blinks. "You do?"

"Don't fall for that. He only 'loves' you now because it's convenient," Sherry butts in. "If he brokers a hotel deal on this property, it will make him more money in one transaction than you or I will ever see in our lives. And he's too smart not to know that his best chance of convincing Erma and Dean to sell is wooing you."

"That's bullshit." I whirl on her. "You don't know me, my intentions, or my heart. You don't know a fucking thing."

Sherry glares at me. "Are you going to tell me you had no idea the Abelsons have all but given Skye this property?"

I can't say that. "You have everything wrong. A client asked me to make inquiries while I was in town. I haven't heard from him in weeks. I'm not pursuing it. And for all I know, he dropped the project. It happens all the time."

"So you just happened to rent this house and then the client asked you to investigate the land?"

No, and I'm not going to put myself in the guilty corner Sherry is trying to push me into. I'm aware that, when it comes to this situation, I have dirt under my nails. But no fucking way am I admitting to the premeditated screwing she's trying to pin on me.

"Sherry, no matter how bad you paint me to be, even if you manage to separate me from the mother of my child for your own selfish ends— which is really despicable, in my opinion—Skye isn't going to fall madly in love with Finn. And he isn't going to leave his wife for her. Instead of trying to make everyone do what you want them to, why don't you work on accepting what is?"

The woman gasps, wide eyed, pressing her hand to her chest as if she's a delicate little flower and I'm the sun brutally wilting her away.

I don't give a shit. She and her act both piss me off.

Ignoring her, I take Skye by the elbow. "Let's go inside and talk about this, honey."

She digs in her heels. "Did you stay here specifically to check out the property?"

I can't lie to her. "Yes, but that has nothing to do with why I remained or why I wanted you."

She stares at me, weighing my words. I can't tell if she believes me. "Did you know that the Abelsons intend to leave me this property someday?"

This is a trickier question.

I sigh. I didn't owe Sherry a damn thing, but I owe Skye this answer. I can't build any kind of future with her or our baby if I'm not honest. "The night we went to Nia's for dinner, Maxon told me he'd heard that rumor, but he didn't know if it was true. I never followed up because it didn't matter to me. I love you."

She looks unmoved by my declaration. "But you also weren't honest with me. You never mentioned a client or a potential hotel deal or due diligence for either. You told me about your dad and your sisters, your concussion, and your sad New York life—all the things designed to pull on my heartstrings."

"And every word I said was true."

"Just not the whole truth. You said you'd always do your best to give me honesty, and that turned out to be a lie. I should have listened to my gut about you, slick."

Her words crush my hope—and my heart. But I try not to panic. Life has tossed Skye a lot today. She was undoubtedly shocked to discover she was pregnant. Just like she was surely stunned to hear that I "betrayed" her. She's understandably conflicted and confused as hell. And for all I know, her hormones are raging, too. I need to keep my cool.

"Skye… I'm sorry. I'm so fucking sorry, honey. I couldn't betray a client's confidence, and—"

"But you could betray me." Her mouth purses, and something so angry darkens her usually soft brown eyes. "Get your things and go."

My chest seizes. I forget how to breathe. I don't ask if she's serious. It's obvious she is.

I reach for her. "Don't do this. We have a baby coming. We need to talk this out. There are things you don't understand."

She wrenches away from me. "I understand enough. We're done."

"We're not." I shake my head. "We're having a child together."

"I don't need anything from you. The baby and I will be just fine." Then she turns to Sherry. "This doesn't mean I'm coming back to Finn or that he's anything more than a friend. You need to let it go. I'm never going to love him the way Dana does. Now I'd like to be alone."

She turns away, and I watch her walk up the hill toward her little one-room cottage. For one of the few times in my life, I'm at a loss for words. In the span of one afternoon, I went from thinking I had endless possibilities to nearly having everything meaningful taken from me.

What the fuck do I do now?

I turn to Sherry, who actually looks somewhere between confused and contrite. "You're no good for her."

"That's not your decision. I love her in a way your son never will. I would have loved her for the rest of my life if you hadn't stuck your big mouth in our business. I hope you can live with the fact that she may be raising a child alone because you're a selfish bitch."

Then I walk away because I have nothing more to say. My heart hurts so fucking bad I'm shocked my chest isn't bleeding out. But I also know I'm not giving up on Skye.

CHAPTER FIVE

Monday, February 5

"Can I talk to you?"

Finn swivels his head around from the big-screen above the wide bar in the middle of the swanky Lahaina hotel. His eyes narrow when he sees me. "You're still on the island? I thought you'd be back in New York."

He tone makes it clear he'd prefer that.

I shake my head. "I'm not going anywhere."

"Whatever. You're an asshole. I've got nothing to say to you."

I've got plenty to say to him. I've spent the last two days trying to get a hold of Skye. I texted and called. No answer. I left voicemails. No response. I even drove back out to the Aloha Rainbow house, but the gate barring the private road was locked shut. I thought about scaling it and insisting she listen to me. I didn't. She's telling me without words that she doesn't want to talk. I've bungled everything like an idiot, rationalizing all my actions and basically shoving my head up my ass for the last month.

After a lot of soul searching, it's time to make things between us right.

Finn is my last hope.

A couple of tourists beside him order fruity drinks and eye us, so I choose my words carefully. "You don't know my side of this, and she won't hear me right now. Is there someplace we can talk privately?"

"No." He focuses on the TV again.

"Please."

"How the fuck did you find me?"

"I remembered where your wife works. I asked her how I could find you." And after a sufficient amount of pleading and groveling, she told me, thank god.

"Damn Dana's soft heart." Finn shakes his head, but I know he wouldn't have her any other way.

"She took pity on me. I'm hoping I can convince you to do the same."

He sends me an exasperated glare. "Look, Skye can't take any more, and I'm going to protect her. That's the least I can do. She only got personal with you because I was the stupid asshole who pressured her into finding a fake fiancé for my wedding. What I should have done was tell my mother to back the hell off. Trust me, I rectified the situation yesterday."

That's good news. Finn is a grown man who should have long ago made his mom butt out of his love life. Hopefully, she's gotten the message.

"She any better with Dana now?"

He looks startled by my question. "Like you give a shit?"

"Yeah. Your happiness is important to Skye. She feels terrible that your mom has been so fixated on her taking Dana's place in your life."

Finn huffs, obviously sick of it, too. "It's a little better. But the whole situation will take time. You, um…know that Skye and I were never really a thing, right?"

Since his anger has come down a notch, I slide onto the empty stool beside him. "Yeah. But I also know she considers you one of her best friends."

His face softens, and he motions to the bartender for another beer, then looks at me in question. "Same."

I shake my head to decline the drink and wait until the dude in the logoed tank top slides a cold one in Finn's direction before I go in for the kill. "That means you have sway with Skye. And I'm hoping that, since you're such good friends, you want her to be happy, too."

Finn glares at me. "That's low."

Because he does want to see her happy and he's figured out that I want his help in winning her back.

"I'm willing to do anything. Name it."

"Even give up the deal you tried to sell her down the river for?"

"Already done."

I called David Chang within an hour of Skye tossing me out of the Aloha Rainbow house. Despite it being Sunday in Hong Kong, I rang him up and explained that the land belongs to an older couple who will never sell because they're leaving it to a girl who's like family to them. And no, I won't apply pressure to her because I'm hoping to make her my wife.

David was stunned silent for a long moment before he laughed and agreed to look harder at some of the other properties I'd sent his way. I committed to helping him as long as he didn't expect me to work against Skye's wishes. He also said he had a lot of other opportunities for me to consider all through Hawaii, the South Pacific, and Asia, if I was game.

I am. And I took that information to my dad. Then he and I talked. I have a plan for the future now. But it all hinges on Skye—and whether I can convince her ex to persuade her to talk to me.

Finn blinks at me. "You actually walked away from a multimillion-dollar deal for your fake fiancée? Despite the fact you've known each other for less than a month?"

I nod. "There will be other deals, but Skye is one of a kind. What we have may have started as pretend, but I love her. I've never said that about any woman in my life."

"What supposedly changed, brah?"

"Everything. You know that."

"I know she's pregnant. Good job, asshole. And if you only want her because you knocked her up—"

"No. I was already thinking about our future when she gave me the news."

He scoffs. "Well, dream on. Even if she was speaking to you, she would *never* move to New York. And if she went to make you happy, it would tear her up."

"I know." Which is why I know exactly what I have to do. "I just want to talk to her. Please." When Finn still looks unmoved, I lean in and press on. "Look, you stood strong and married the woman you love, even when some of the most important people in your life were against it. You followed your heart. I need a chance to tell Skye what's in mine. Ten minutes. That's all I'm asking."

Yeah, he's not thrilled, but Finn finally sighs. "God, I must be a sucker. But let's be clear, I'm only saying yes and risking my friendship with Skye because she's miserable and I'm convinced she loves you, too."

He drops his voice again. "If you fuck her over again, though? I'll make sure you piss through a straw for the rest of your goddamn life."

He has absolutely no way to make that a reality, and we both know it. But if it makes him feel better to believe he's got some leverage over me, fine. I will totally bend my pride. "Absolutely, but I won't."

"When and where?"

"Any time and place of her choosing between now and Friday." I'm as accommodating as I can be.

Finn nods. We exchange numbers, and he says he'll be in touch. After that, there's nothing to say. I have to find my fucking patience somehow, scramble to get everything in place, and hope like hell it's enough.

Because I already know I'll never love anyone else the way I love shy, quirky, big-hearted Skye Ingram.

CHAPTER SIX

Friday, February 9
Skye

It's been exactly one month since Stephen Lund crashed into my life. In thirty short days, he's changed it completely. Then again, I never imagined for a moment that the guy who offered to take me to Finn's wedding—the one who made my head spin and my heart race—had ulterior motives. I still don't know the whole truth, but after six days of stewing and wondering, one thing is clear: We need to talk. Finn is right about that.

What happens today will decide everything.

Nervously, I smooth down the floral print skirt of my dress as the valet takes my car. Then I step into the open breezeway of the Four Seasons.

I'm so confused right now I'm not even sure what to hope for, but Stephen has a ticket on a flight off the island tomorrow. He has since the day I met him. So it's now or never for this conversation. Unfortunately, I had to wait until nearly sunset before my stomach settled. In the past week, I've learned that mornings and pregnancy hormones don't always mix well.

In my purse, my phone vibrates. I pull it from my clutch to see an encouraging text from Finn. After sending back my thanks, I tuck the device away.

Thank god he's been such a steady friend. Without him and Dana, I would have been so lost.

The evening I kicked Stephen to the curb, the house we'd shared for three amazing weeks felt empty and ghost-filled. I've worked there for six years. Erma and Dean have promised that it's my future. And for the first time I couldn't stand to be inside those four walls.

I'd known I was falling for Stephen fast and hard, but I didn't realize how wretchedly in love I was until he was gone. Until I slept in our bed to be near him and smelled him on our sheets. Until I remembered all the laughter, flirtation, and pleasure we shared. Until his absence ripped me in half, leaving me incomplete, bleeding, and alone.

When I called Finn, he and Dana came running, held me while I sobbed, and listened through all my tears. They've been great. They've held my hands. They especially encouraged me to call my parents and tell them everything. Finn knew it would make me feel better. He was right.

I worked up the courage to pick up the phone the next morning. My parents were understandably shocked by my pregnancy, but supportive of whatever I choose to do. I'm not precisely sure how I'll juggle being a mom, but I don't need to know that today. I need to figure out my next steps with Stephen first. As much as the hurt part of me wants to curse him and cut him cold out of spite, this is his child, too. And if he doesn't want anything to do with our baby, it's his loss.

If he writes off both me and his kid, that will prove that Sherry was right—and hurt so damn bad.

But even knowing that's a distinct possibility, my stupid heart refuses to love him any less.

So here I am, at the Four Seasons, wearing a dress that feels more like armor, to settle this. There are too many memories at Aloha Rainbow. If we'd talked there, I'm not sure I would have been able to stop myself from begging him for just one more idyllic night in his arms.

My heels click across the tile floors of the elegant open-air lobby, decorated mostly in muted tans and creams with lots of greenery, illuminated by classic wrought-iron light fixtures. My heart clatters even faster than my footsteps, so fast I swear it's pounding out of my chest. By the time I reach the elevator, I'm trembling visibly. It's tough to catch my breath on the ride up to the top floor.

I step out of the car, and a quick glance at the plaque tells me Stephen's suite is at the end of the hall to my right. All I have to do is find the courage to make my way down there and knock.

Why does he want to see me? The question has been haunting me for two days, since Finn persuaded me this meeting is necessary. Is this his last-ditch attempt to get his hands on Erma and Dean's land? Or does he want to buy me off so he doesn't have to bother with anything as pesky as fatherhood?

That doesn't seem like the man I know...but did I know him at all? And if he really is that asshole, I'll handle the future alone. I'm strong. Sure, I want Stephen Lund—more than I thought possible after only knowing him for a handful of weeks. But if he bails, I will survive.

I have to.

The thought bolsters me as I trek to the end of the hallway.

What if he tells you he loves you again?

My footsteps falter. I don't have an answer for that. And after everything that's passed, how could I ever believe him again?

I press a hand to my unsettled stomach and knock.

When the door opens, I'm shocked to find the senior Lund standing there, wearing a Hawaiian shirt, a pressed pair of khakis, and a kind smile. "Hi, Skye. Good to see you again. Come in."

"Mr. Lund." I nod politely and ease inside, lip-biting and stiff.

I can only imagine what this man must be thinking...

"Call me Douglas," he invites, shaking my hand in a warm clasp between both of his. "Please, sit."

I peek through the entryway, into a sitting room that's bigger than the caretaker's cottage I live in. It's understated and lovely, with a view of the ocean that is absolutely breathtaking. What I don't see is Stephen.

Did he change his mind?

"I'm fine, thank you."

"Bottle of water? Soda? I'd offer you something with teeth but..."

I'm pregnant, and he knows it. Besides, I'm not sure I'll be here long enough to drink anything. "No, thank you."

"If you change your mind, there's a mini-fridge behind the bar. Help yourself to whatever you want." He tosses me a smile. "But it's a good thing you can't drink Scotch. Stephen already availed himself of it all the night he left you. Thank you for coming to put him out of his misery."

Misery? Because his deal isn't going through? "Thank you for letting us meet here."

What else can I say?

"Stephen will be just a minute more. He's thrilled you're willing to talk." I'm surprised when Douglas's smile widens. "When it's all said and done, I think you're going to be happy, too. I sincerely hope I'll see you again very soon."

With a tip of his head, he exits the suite and leaves me completely confused. For two days, I've had visions of this powerful Wall Street mogul berating me. I thought he'd accuse me of getting pregnant on purpose and call me a gold digger. Instead, he went out of his way to be warm and welcoming.

What the heck is happening right now?

I resist the urge to pace to the window and look out at the sun setting over the shimmering Pacific. I want to be braced for the moment the suite's interior door opens and Stephen steps out. I have a speech rehearsed. I'm staying focused on the baby and being an adult about our parenting arrangement. Deep down, would I like to know if any of the romance between us was real? Sure. But I'm not asking. Is it really important anymore?

My heart says it is. It has no sense; I'm not listening.

As the sun sinks closer to the horizon, the door opens to my right. I whirl around. The sight of Stephen Lund in an impeccable gray suit knocks the breath out of me. When those bright blue eyes of his fall on me, I can hardly speak.

I need to be practical, not star struck, damn it.

"Skye. Thank you for agreeing to see me." He gestures me into the rest of the suite, where there's a massive living/dining room with more panoramic views. There are fresh roses on the table. Two glasses of cold bubbling liquid beside a bottle of sparkling cider. The lights are low. We're completely alone.

It feels terrifyingly romantic.

I put on my best business face. "I thought it was important that we talk. I have a custody arrangement in mind. I wrote my ideas up so you can look—"

He stops me from digging into my clutch. "Before you go there, I have a few things I'd like to say. First, I didn't romance you for the property. I need you to know that."

"You already said that. And I'm just supposed to believe you?"

"No. Someday I hope you'll trust what I tell you, but I know today isn't that day. So I'm going to prove it." He withdraws some papers from the pocket of his jacket and hands them to me. "These are generally considered confidential, but I have David Chang's blessing to share them with you. It's an e-mail string. Would you mind reading it? Start at the bottom."

I'm not entirely sure what he thinks this will accomplish, but I admit I'm curious. "All right."

Three minutes later, I'm blinking and struggling to take it all in. But one fact is completely clear: Stephen tried his damnedest for weeks to tempt Chang with other properties besides my beloved Aloha Rainbow.

"This is real?"

"One-hundred percent. I'll be happy to pull it up on my phone, if you'd like to validate."

The evidence seems so black and white. I can only think of one reason he's so insistent to prove his point. Hope sparks bright and dangerous.

If Stephen wasn't lying about wooing me for the property, what else wasn't he lying about?

I fold up the paper and hand it back to him, my thoughts racing. "You think I jumped to conclusions?"

"The natural one, given what Sherry was spewing. And I'll fully admit that for my first day or two at Aloha Rainbow, I didn't care much what happened to the place. It would have been a great deal for me. I would have made bank while I gained professional independence from my father. And if that had to happen on someone else's back…" He shrugs. "Well, that's business. Then I got to know you."

"Why bother trying to convince me that I matter now? I'm here to offer you really liberal visitation, so if that's what you're after…"

"Fuck visitation."

I suck in a breath. So Stephen wants more. Like pie-in-the-sky more?

He crooks a finger at me. "Come here, honey."

My stomach pitches and tightens again. "What do you want?"

"Dance with me."

Of all the things he could have said, I didn't see that one coming. Now I'm really nervous. And way more excited than I want to admit. "Why? There's no music."

He holds up a finger, withdraws his phone from his pocket, and launches a soft, sultry R&B tune before he reaches out and takes me in his arms.

Honestly, I never imagined being this close to Stephen Lund again. But he presses me into his body, then begins dancing with me—slow smooth, sensual. Being this close to him is heaven.

I can't help myself; I sigh into him. I fill my nose with him. I cuddle close and revel in his hardness everywhere I'm soft. I prove just how horribly weak I am when it comes to this man—and in the moment, I just don't care.

"I don't want to visit my child any more than I want to visit you," he murmurs against my ear.

A shiver zips down my spine. "Then what do you want?"

"You said once that you'd rather go through the hard times with someone you love than have a perfectly carefree life alone. I've lived that easy-breezy, pointless life of solitude. Being with you for those three amazing weeks taught me that I want more. Don't make me settle for less."

I hold my breath. "What are you saying?"

"I want more. I want everything. I want you."

"Stephen, I—"

He lays a finger over my lips. "I'm not done. Let me finish."

The song fades out, and Bruno Mars fills the speakers, crooning about getting married. The same song we danced to at Finn and Dana's wedding. It brings back a happy memory of the night I really fell for Stephen. I can't hear this tune and not think about him, about us.

If we had a song, this would be it.

"What are you doing?"

He cups my cheek and delves into my eyes. "What I've wanted to for a while. Hear me out. I deserve that much since you lied to me."

I gape at him. "No, I didn't."

"You did." A slow smile stretches across his face, somehow playful and sexy at once. "You said we didn't have a song, that you weren't that kind of girl. But the second this song came on just now, your face softened, you held me tighter, and your lips parted as if you were inviting me to kiss you."

Though he's not wrong, I could cling to my pride and protest again. But I'm dying to know what he's up to. "What's your point?"

"You have no idea how badly I want to take you up on that invitation."

Given the hot suggestion in his eyes, I think I do. The same answering note flares in my belly. "That doesn't make this our song."

"I want it to be." He strokes a soft thumb across my cheek. "I'm hoping to make it ours."

Then he gets down on one knee.

My eyes widen and I gasp when he pulls a little box from his pocket, flips it open to reveal a sparkling ring that's very real and even more beautiful than the fake, then smiles up at me with hope all over his face.

"Skye Nicole Ingram, we've only known each other for a month. But I don't need longer to know that you make me smile, make me think, and—I admit—make me want to kiss you breathless for the rest of our lives. You amuse, befuddle, and intrigue me. Most of all, you made me fall madly in love with you. If you say yes, I'll be the best fiancé—and husband—ever, listening, laughing, and loving you, from now until death do us part. Will you do me the very real honor of marrying me?"

His words are an echo of the playful proposal he uttered shortly after we met. But this speech is solemn and heartfelt. His eyes will me to say yes.

What's left of my anger dissipates. I blink, struggle to breathe. My heart clutches inside my chest.

"Say something, Skye. I turned down my dad's offer to run Colossus for you. He'll continue helming the company, and I'll relocate here to start a new subsidiary that specializes in Asian and Pacific interests so I can be with you. I made plans for us to elope to Vegas. All I'm asking in return is one little word. Just say yes."

I'm so touched, I can't speak. Stephen blurs in my vision. My throat closes up. How can I possibly say no? I love this man. I've loved him almost from the beginning.

"You sacrificed everything?" His deal, his dream job, and his home. All for me.

He really does love me. I blink, and the tears fall down my face.

Stephen stands, towers over me, and cups my face. "I've sacrificed nothing if I can have you as my wife. Before I met you, I carefully orchestrated everything in my life, but my whole existence had no meaning. I didn't plan to fall in love with you, but you opened my eyes. You showed me what I've been missing. Falling for you was the best thing I've ever done."

There's only one thing I can say, but it's not easy through my tears. "Yes."

He grips me tighter. "Yes, you'll marry me?"

I smile. "Yes. I'll marry you. I love you."

He laughs as he yanks the ring out of the box and quickly slides it on my finger. "Honey, I love you, too. More than anything."

We're engaged—for real. I can't believe it. More happy tears fall. He swipes them away with his thumbs before he kisses me breathless, reminding me of just one of the many reasons I've never been able to resist this man.

As I melt into him, he eases away and glances at his watch. "How soon can you be packed?"

I'm confused. "For what? To spend a few days here with you?"

He shakes his head. "Our flight to Vegas leaves in three hours."

"What?"

"I figured you'd like something spontaneous…"

He's not meticulously planning our wedding? "I don't have a dress."

"We'll get you one."

"That takes time. Weeks. Months, even."

He winks at me. "Not when you have money."

"But we haven't invited anyone."

"Who do you want there?"

He's making this sound so simple. "My parents. Finn and Dana. Erma and Dean." That's it. Those are the most important people in my life.

"I'll get them there ASAP, along with my dad, Amanda, Bethany, Nia and Evan. Beyond that, I don't need anyone except you."

I'm not sure exactly when this ceremony will take place or where we'll live or how any of the practicalities of our life together will work. But I know I'll have Stephen by my side. "I don't need anyone else, either."

"I'll do everything in my power to make you feel that way for the rest of your life."

Then he smiles down at me and cements that vow with a kiss that holds all the promise of our tomorrows.

* * * *

Also from 1001 Dark Nights and Shayla Black, discover More Than Protect You, Dirty Wicked, Forever Wicked and Pure Wicked.

Sign up for the 1001 Dark Nights Newsletter
and be entered to win a Tiffany Key necklace.

There's a contest every month!

Go to www.1001DarkNights.com to subscribe.

**As a bonus, all subscribers can download
FIVE FREE exclusive books!**

DISCOVER 1001 DARK NIGHTS COLLECTION SIX

DRAGON CLAIMED by Donna Grant
A Dark Kings Novella

ASHES TO INK by Carrie Ann Ryan
A Montgomery Ink: Colorado Springs Novella

ENSNARED by Elisabeth Naughton
An Eternal Guardians Novella

EVERMORE by Corinne Michaels
A Salvation Series Novella

VENGEANCE by Rebecca Zanetti
A Dark Protectors/Rebels Novella

ELI'S TRIUMPH by Joanna Wylde
A Reapers MC Novella

CIPHER by Larissa Ione
A Demonica Underworld Novella

RESCUING MACIE by Susan Stoker
A Delta Force Heroes Novella

ENCHANTED by Lexi Blake
A Masters and Mercenaries Novella

TAKE THE BRIDE by Carly Phillips
A Knight Brothers Novella

INDULGE ME by J. Kenner
A Stark Ever After Novella

THE KING by Jennifer L. Armentrout
A Wicked Novella

QUIET MAN by Kristen Ashley
A Dream Man Novella

ABANDON by Rachel Van Dyken
A Seaside Pictures Novella

THE OPEN DOOR by Laurelin Paige
A Found Duet Novella

CLOSER by Kylie Scott
A Stage Dive Novella

SOMETHING JUST LIKE THIS by Jennifer Probst
A Stay Novella

BLOOD NIGHT by Heather Graham
A Krewe of Hunters Novella

TWIST OF FATE by Jill Shalvis
A Heartbreaker Bay Novella

MORE THAN PLEASURE YOU by Shayla Black
A More Than Words Novella

WONDER WITH ME by Kristen Proby
A With Me In Seattle Novella

THE DARKEST ASSASSIN by Gena Showalter
A Lords of the Underworld Novella

Also from 1001 Dark Nights:
DAMIEN by J. Kenner

DISCOVER MORE SHAYLA BLACK

More Than Protect You: **A More Than Words Novella**
By Shayla Black
Coming October 6, 2019

Can I keep the gorgeous, gun-shy single mother safe—and prove I'm the man for her?

I'm Tanner Kirk—Certified firearms instructor and mixed martial arts enthusiast. When I filed for divorce at the end of an empty marriage, all I wanted was a vacation in paradise, not another woman in my life. But how can I possibly say no to Amanda Lund, a young single mom desperate to learn self-defense? Or refuse the banked desire on the guarded beauty's face?

I can't.

So I seduce Mandy until we're burning up the sheets…and soon find my heart entangled with her bruised and battered one. But when a nemesis from her past tries to destroy our future by unearthing my secret, will she understand and forgive me—or give up on us forever?

* * * *

Dirty Wicked: **A Wicked Lovers Novella**
By Shayla Black

After being framed for a crime he didn't commit, former private eye Nick Navarro has nothing but revenge on his mind—until a woman from his past returns to beg for his help.

Beautiful widow Sasha Porter has been hunted by his enemies. Desperate, she offers him anything to keep her young daughter safe, even agreeing to become his mistress. The last thing either of them want are emotional entanglements but as they entrap the ruthless politician who arranged Nick's downfall and passion sizzles between them, danger closes in.

Will he choose love over vengeance before it's too late?

* * * *

Forever Wicked: A Wicked Lovers Novella
By Shayla Black

They had nothing in common but a desperate passion…

Billionaire Jason Denning lived life fast and hard in a world where anything could be bought and sold, even affection. But all that changed when he met "Greta," a beautiful stranger ready to explore her hidden desires. From a blue collar family, Gia Angelotti wore a badge, fought for right—and opened herself utterly to love him. Blindsided and falling hard, Jason does the first impulsive thing of his life and hustles her to the altar.

Until a second chance proved that forever could be theirs.

Then tragedy ripped Jason's new bride from his arms and out of his life. When he finds Gia again, he gives her a choice: spend the three weeks before their first anniversary with him or forfeit the money she receives from their marriage. Reluctantly, she agrees to once again put herself at his mercy and return to his bed. But having her right where he wants her is dangerous for Jason's peace of mind. No matter how hard he tries, he finds himself falling for her again. Will he learn to trust that their love is real before Gia leaves again for good?

* * * *

Pure Wicked: A Wicked Lovers Novella
By Shayla Black

During his decade as an international pop star, Jesse McCall has lived every day in the fast lane. A committed hedonist reveling in amazing highs, globetrotting, and nameless encounters, he refuses to think about his loneliness or empty future. Then tragedy strikes.

Shocked and grieving, he sheds his identity and walks away, searching for peace. Instead, he finds Bristol Reese, a no-nonsense beauty scraping to keep her business afloat while struggling with her own demons. He's intent on seducing her, but other than a pleasure-filled night, she's not interested in a player, especially after her boyfriend recently proposed to her sister. In order to claim Bristol, Jesse has to prove he's not the kind of man he's always been. But when she learns his identity and his past comes back to haunt him, how will he convince her that he's a changed man who wants nothing more than to make her his forever?

MORE THAN WANT YOU
More Than Words series, book 1
By Shayla Black

What starts as sweet revenge against Maxon's most savage competitor—his brother—becomes an unquenchable hunger for Keeley, the sassy free spirit he hires to trip up his enemy.

"So you have to beat the champ at his own game." Rob sighs, sounding like he finally understands my proclamation that I'm fucked.

There's no way to top Griff. He's got a goddamn natural gift.

"Okay, your brother might find a buyer a week or two earlier." Britta shrugs. "But you're the better man."

"They don't give a shit about that."

"You always come through," she argues.

"To the people dying to unload this estate so they can cash out, those seven days make a five-figure difference in their bank account. Besides, they don't know the Maui market. And they don't know me except as the pushy salesman who barged in. They certainly don't know my reputation except through boring statistics and my own claims, which they probably see as bragging. It sounds as if Susan Stowe was fond of Griff, so she picked him. Her heirs would need a damn good reason to cross her wishes."

My brother would have to fuck up badly. And he never does. Well, almost never…unless there's a gorgeous woman involved. Unlike me, he has a bad habit of allowing his dick to distract him. Always has. That's how he started fooling around with Britta at the office once upon a time. Too bad he's not having a torrid fuckfest with someone high maintenance now—at least not according to my spies. A good hourglass-shaped distraction in Griff's bed would sure help my cause.

As the waitress sets down our drinks, the lights dim. Everyone turns to the stage at one end of the cramped sports bar. Ah, the live entertainment. After the tragic act last week, I was hoping we would miss the show.

But then I see *her*.

Crooked smile. Pink hair. Winged black liner over laughing blue eyes. Vivid red lipstick. Tacky cheetah-print dress. Tiny waist. Sleek legs.

Chunky black heels that have seen better days. I don't think I would have looked at her twice normally, but she's got two things going for her: an obvious zest for life and a great rack.

Griff can't resist either.

I turn in my chair to watch as she grabs the microphone with deft confidence. She's comfortable on stage.

"Aloha, Lahaina. I'm Keeley Sunshine. I'm going to sing you some of my favorite songs, and since I'm a single girl in the middle of a long drought, they'll probably all be about sex. You can buy me drinks after the set if you'd like to change that." She winks.

She's got a certain charm. Griff values that, along with a sense of humor.

"I'd be more than happy to end her drought," Rob whispers in my ear as the small band nods at one another.

Keeley Sunshine—clearly not her real name—closes her eyes as the primal beat of the music rises to a quirky old tune. It's familiar. I know I've heard the song but I'm having trouble placing it, until the chorus. Then, while she sways her hips to the beat, she's belting out that she doesn't want anybody else. She just thinks about me and touches herself.

Oh, yeah.

Less than thirty seconds; that's how long it takes me to have my first boner for her. And I'm a tough customer. At thirty-three, I'm not used to adjusting my dick or embarrassing myself around a girl. That stuff happened, like, fifteen years ago.

As she deftly transitions to the second verse, I picture her naked, pretty tits pointing at the ceiling, legs in the air. In my head, she's got a bare pussy, which I realize may not be accurate, but that's how she looks in fantasy. Griff likes them smooth, too—about the only thing we agree on anymore.

When Keeley assures everyone in the room she would get down on her knees and do anything for whomever she's singing to, she's not looking at anyone in particular.

She ought to be looking at me.

But she seems lost in the song, in her passion for the music. She's got a surprisingly smooth voice with just a hint of rasp. Another check in her plus column.

As the song winds toward the end, her oohs and aahs grow breathier and louder, higher-pitched. Shit, she's having a choral orgasm center stage. And yeah, I squirm, fighting the urge to pry my hard dick off the teeth of my zipper. I can't help it. I'm a guy, and Keeley Sunshine drips sex.

The old Divinyls classic ends to hearty applause. I have to agree that this vixen is a musical savant compared to last week's squeaky screen door on repeat. At a tap of Keeley's toe—I notice her nail polish is black—the band begins the next tune.

Old jazz, the kind you drink to, so easy it makes you smile. But they've modernized it with guitars and drums. Still, I know this tune well because my granddad loved it. Eddie Cantor's 1929 classic "Makin' Whoopee." But she sings it like Rachel MacFarlane, smooth and vampy.

I gotta admit, I'm mesmerized. I can't stop watching her mouth. Her lips are bee-stung and would look great wrapped around a cock. Mine, for instance.

When the jazz standard ends to even more enthusiastic applause, Keeley picks another decades-old tune. I suspect she's got an old soul. It fits her slightly retro vibe.

After a sexy, rhythmic intro, she drags in a deep breath, nearly kissing the mic, and uses her breathy voice to say that she put a spell on me because I'm hers. Right now, I can't argue, especially when her words sparkle brighter than glitter.

Listening to her, I get chills.

Britta leans closer, lips near my ear. "Put your tongue back in your mouth."

I shoot her a quelling glance, but she's right. Under normal circumstances, I'd wait for Keeley Sunshine's set to end, buy her a strong drink, and sweet-talk my way into her panties for the night. But right now the needs of my business outweigh the needs of my dick.

If Griff could see this woman, especially if I cleaned her up a bit, he'd be all over her. In fact, that's a great idea. I need to figure out how to hook the two of them up—fast—so he stops thinking about the Stowe estate with all those beachfront views.

Still, I can't suggest that to Britta without upsetting her.

"Blow me," I murmur instead.

Britta scoffs. "No, thanks. You're an asshole."

"I am." That's something I'm proud of. Best way to get ahead in business.

"It runs in the Reed family."

She's right. My old man is an impeccable textbook example of a puckered anus, too. From him, I learned well. Vaguely, I wonder which pretty young thing he's banging in his office while my mom buries her head in some all-talk/no-action ladies' function, but they've moved to San Diego. It's no longer my problem. I'm only irritated they took my younger sister but didn't persuade Griff to shove off with them. He's a total sphincter.

Keeley hits and holds a growly high note that demands my attention. Her voice sneaks behind my fly and wraps around my cock. Her puffy lips are mobile and soft. Her dress exaggerates the womanly curve of her hips, which she swings as she roars out the last note.

I might have thought I wouldn't look at her twice, but that's bullshit. I could definitely listen to her for hours. And I think I could do her all night long.

As her final note trails off, the applause is even louder, like the audience has realized she's pretty damn amazing.

She blushes as she laughs off our reaction. Her smile quickly proves to be the most beautiful thing about her. White, blinding, real. She's enjoying the crowd and yet seems almost surprised by their enthusiasm.

With a swing of her long pink hair, her curls catch the light, then fall gracefully over her shoulders. She shrugs at her guitar player, an old man who looks impressed.

"This will be our last song for the set. If you have requests, write them down and leave them in the jar." She points to the clear vessel at her feet. "We'll be back to play in thirty. If you have a dirty proposition, I'll entertain them at the bar in five." She says the words like she's kidding.

I, however, am totally serious.

Keeley starts her next song, a more recent pop tune, in a breathy, a capella murmur. "Can't keep my hands to myself."

She taps her thigh in a rhythm only she can hear until the band joins during the crescendo to the chorus. Keeley bounces her way through the lyrics with a flirty smile. It's both alluring and fun, a tease of a song.

Though I rarely smile, I find myself grinning along.

As she finishes, I glance around. There's more than one hungry dog with a bone in this damn bar.

I didn't get ahead in business or life by being polite or waiting my turn. She hasn't even wrapped her vocal cords around the last note but I'm on my feet and charging across the room.

I'm the first one to reach the corner of the bar closest to the stage. I prop my elbow on the slightly sticky wood to claim my territory, then glare back at the three other men who think they should end Keeley's supposed sex drought. They are not watering her garden, and my snarl makes that clear.

One sees my face, stops in his tracks, and immediately backs off. Smart man.

Number Two looks like a smarmy car salesman. He rakes Keeley up and down with his gaze like she's a slab of beef, but she's flirting my way as she tucks her mic on its stand. I smile back.

She's not really my type, but man, I'd love to hit that.

Out of the corner of my eye, I watch the approaching dirtbag finger his porn 'stouche. To stake my claim, I reach out to help Keeley off the stage. She looks pleasantly surprised by my gesture as she wraps her fingers around mine.

I can be a gentleman…when it suits me.

Fuck, she's warm and velvety, and her touch makes my cock jolt. Her second would-be one-night stand curses then slinks back to his seat.

That leaves me to fend off Number Three. He looks like a WWE reject—hulking and hit in the face too many times. If she prefers brawn over brains, I'll have to find another D-cup distraction for Griff.

That would truly suck. My gut tells me Keeley is perfect for the job.

Would it be really awful if I slept with her before I introduced her to my brother?

ABOUT SHAYLA BLACK

Shayla Black is the *New York Times* and *USA Today* bestselling author of nearly eighty novels. For over twenty years, she's written contemporary, erotic, paranormal, and historical romances via traditional, independent, foreign, and audio publishers. Her books have sold several million copies and been published in a dozen languages.

Raised an only child, Shayla occupied herself with lots of daydreaming, much to the chagrin of her teachers. In college, she found her love for reading and realized that she could have a career publishing the stories spinning in her imagination. Though she graduated with a degree in Marketing/Advertising and embarked on a stint in corporate America to pay the bills, her heart has always been with her characters. She's thrilled that she's been living her dream as a full-time author for the past eleven years.

Shayla currently lives in North Texas with her wonderfully supportive husband, her daughter, and two spoiled tabbies. In her "free" time, she enjoys reality TV, reading, and listening to an eclectic blend of music.

Connect with me online:
Website: http://shaylablack.com
Newsletter: http://shayla.link/nwsltr
Facebook: http://shayla.link/FBPage
FB Chat Group: http://shayla.link/FBChat
Instagram: http://shayla.link/IG
Book+Main Bites: http://shayla.link/books+main
Goodreads: http://shayla.link/Goodreads
Twitter: http://shayla.link/Twitter
Pinterest: http://shayla.link/Pinterest
YouTube: http://shayla.link/YouTube
BookBub: http://shayla.link/BookBub
Amazon: http://shayla.link/AmazonFollow
Text: Text "Shayla" to 24587

If you enjoyed this book, I would appreciate your help so others can enjoy it, too.

Recommend it. Please help other readers find this book by recommending it to friends, readers' groups and discussion boards.

Review it. Please tell other readers why you liked this book by reviewing it at the book retailer of your choice. Thank you!

DISCOVER 1001 DARK NIGHTS

COLLECTION ONE
FOREVER WICKED by Shayla Black
CRIMSON TWILIGHT by Heather Graham
CAPTURED IN SURRENDER by Liliana Hart
SILENT BITE: A SCANGUARDS WEDDING by Tina Folsom
DUNGEON GAMES by Lexi Blake
AZAGOTH by Larissa Ione
NEED YOU NOW by Lisa Renee Jones
SHOW ME, BABY by Cherise Sinclair
ROPED IN by Lorelei James
TEMPTED BY MIDNIGHT by Lara Adrian
THE FLAME by Christopher Rice
CARESS OF DARKNESS by Julie Kenner

COLLECTION TWO
WICKED WOLF by Carrie Ann Ryan
WHEN IRISH EYES ARE HAUNTING by Heather Graham
EASY WITH YOU by Kristen Proby
MASTER OF FREEDOM by Cherise Sinclair
CARESS OF PLEASURE by Julie Kenner
ADORED by Lexi Blake
HADES by Larissa Ione
RAVAGED by Elisabeth Naughton
DREAM OF YOU by Jennifer L. Armentrout
STRIPPED DOWN by Lorelei James
RAGE/KILLIAN by Alexandra Ivy/Laura Wright
DRAGON KING by Donna Grant
PURE WICKED by Shayla Black
HARD AS STEEL by Laura Kaye
STROKE OF MIDNIGHT by Lara Adrian
ALL HALLOWS EVE by Heather Graham
KISS THE FLAME by Christopher Rice
DARING HER LOVE by Melissa Foster
TEASED by Rebecca Zanetti
THE PROMISE OF SURRENDER by Liliana Hart

MIDNIGHT UNLEASHED by Lara Adrian
HALLOW BE THE HAUNT by Heather Graham
DIRTY FILTHY FIX by Laurelin Paige
THE BED MATE by Kendall Ryan
NIGHT GAMES by CD Reiss
NO RESERVATIONS by Kristen Proby
DAWN OF SURRENDER by Liliana Hart

COLLECTION FIVE
BLAZE ERUPTING by Rebecca Zanetti
ROUGH RIDE by Kristen Ashley
HAWKYN by Larissa Ione
RIDE DIRTY by Laura Kaye
ROME'S CHANCE by Joanna Wylde
THE MARRIAGE ARRANGEMENT by Jennifer Probst
SURRENDER by Elisabeth Naughton
INKED NIGHTS by Carrie Ann Ryan
ENVY by Rachel Van Dyken
PROTECTED by Lexi Blake
THE PRINCE by Jennifer L. Armentrout
PLEASE ME by J. Kenner
WOUND TIGHT by Lorelei James
STRONG by Kylie Scott
DRAGON NIGHT by Donna Grant
TEMPTING BROOKE by Kristen Proby
HAUNTED BE THE HOLIDAYS by Heather Graham
CONTROL by K. Bromberg
HUNKY HEARTBREAKER by Kendall Ryan
THE DARKEST CAPTIVE by Gena Showalter

Also from 1001 Dark Nights:

TAME ME by J. Kenner
THE SURRENDER GATE By Christopher Rice
SERVICING THE TARGET By Cherise Sinclair
TEMPT ME by J. Kenner

ON BEHALF OF 1001 DARK NIGHTS,

Liz Berry and M.J. Rose would like to thank ~

Steve Berry
Doug Scofield
Kim Guidroz
Jillian Stein
InkSlinger PR
Dan Slater
Asha Hossain
Chris Graham
Fedora Chen
Kasi Alexander
Jessica Johns
Dylan Stockton
Richard Blake
and Simon Lipskar